WITCH WAY TO ROMANCE & RUIN

THE WITCH WAY MYSTERIES - BOOK 2

JANE HINCHEY

BAYWOLF PRESS

BP

BAYWOLF PRESS

Copyright © 2019 by Jane Hinchey

All rights reserved. No part of this book may be reproduced or used in any way without written permission from the publisher, except as permitted under the Copyright Act 1968.

This is a work of fiction. Any resemblance to actual events, locales, or persons is purely coincidental. Unauthorized use could spark the wrath of supernatural forces - or worse, land you as the next curious case in one of my mysteries!

For Donna, thank you.

AUTHOR'S NOTE

Hey there! Welcome to a whirlwind of whimsy and wonder in my Witch Way Mysteries. If you've got a soft spot for the supernatural, you're in for a real treat.

This is your gateway to a world where magic and mystery intertwine. The Witch Way series has now woven its full tale, but the magic doesn't stop here. For news on my latest adventures and stories, don't forget to sign up for my newsletter.

Janehinchey.com/subscribe

Are you ready to conjure up some fun and unravel a few bewitching puzzles? I'll see you on the other side!

xoxo
Jane

ABOUT THIS BOOK

To win the Decadent Dessert's competition, you have to crack a few eggs.

Gran is gearing up to finally take down the reigning winner of Whitefall Cove's annual Decadent Dessert's competition, only the former victor turns up dead, and Gran is the number one suspect. Now all eyes are on us. How on earth do I keep two feuding covens from outright war, prove Gran's innocence, and keep my new bookstore afloat?

My budding friendship with Detective Jackson Ward is my only recourse, but first I need to get past the prickly defenses of his girlfriend, Police Officer Liliana Miles, and convince Jackson to let me in on the case.

Easier said than done when Gran is flirting up a storm with every male within a ten-mile radius and basking in the spotlight. The hot new lawyer hired to clear her name is not only mysterious but a distraction I don't need, and the witches are misbehaving trying to prove who has more power and spark, which begs the question, can we catch the killer before the next spell is cast?

CHAPTER

ONE

"Oh my god, here he comes! Quick, get out of here." Wendy waddled away from the front window of The Dusty Attic bookstore, hands caressing her swollen belly. I snatched up my bag and was almost home free when the bell over the front door chimed, bringing with it a gust of air and the unmistakable scent of Detective Jackson Ward's cologne. Clutching my bag to my chest, I waited for the inevitable.

"Ah good, you're back." The ghost of Whitney Sims immediately appeared, as she did whenever Jackson and I were together in the store. It appeared his necromancing powers, combined with my witch magic, tethered her to the Dusty Attic. It had been two months since her death and each time she appeared, she didn't seem to notice the discrepancy in time or how long she'd been gone. "I've got more ideas for the book club."

She floated across the floor and a shiver danced up my spine, as it always did whenever she was near. I was new to ghosts and didn't think I'd ever get used to having her around.

"Harper Jones," Jackson drawled, a knowing grin curling the corners of his mouth. "You weren't leaving, were you?"

"I swear to god, you duck in here just to amuse yourself," I grumbled, tossing my bag back behind the desk that served as a counter. Plastering a fake grin on my face, I tuned out Whitney, who was rattling on about the book club and slowly drifting up to the mezzanine level. "What can I do for you, Detective?"

"I hear the book club is reading an Agatha Christie novel this month," he began, nodding a hello to Wendy, who eased herself into the chair behind my desk. "How's it going, Wendy?"

"Despite being the size of a whale and no longer able to see my feet, I'm remarkably well, thank you," she replied, her whole demeanor radiating an Earth-Mother vibe.

I'd taken pity on Wendy when she had to take leave from her job as a nurse, due to her pregnancy. Being on her feet for twelve-hour shifts was too much, so I'd offered her part-time work here at the bookstore. Despite the fact that the ghost of her best friend,

Whitney Sims, haunted the place—and that Wendy had been having an affair with Whitney's husband and was, in fact, carrying his child—it had all turned out remarkably well. It seemed ghost Whitney held no grudges, unlike the living Whitney, who'd been a bully and a terror.

"Yes, we're reading *The A.B.C. Murders*. Why? Did you want to come?"

He shrugged, a sheepish expression flitting across his face.

"Oh! You *do* want to come." My grin widened. "Well, that will make it interesting. You do know I hold the meetings here. And that if I'm here, and you're here..." I trailed off and he filled in the gap.

"Then Whitney will be here."

"Yup. Think you can handle that?"

"You're forgetting I'm a necromancer. I see ghosts everywhere, of course I can handle it."

"Oh really? How come you couldn't see Whitney until that day when my magic leaked through?"

He lifted one shoulder. "Don't know. Who really knows how the afterlife works? But I can tell you that there are no other ghosts inhabiting your store." He seemed pleased to impart that piece of information.

"Anyway, that's not the point. The point is Whitney is going to bug the hell out of the book club members," I pointed out.

"Hey!" Whitney drifted back down to us and stood

with her hands on her hips. "I heard that. And I'd love to sit in on the book club. I promise I'll behave. Please come."

This last comment was directed at Jackson, and she sidled up to him in what I imagined was meant to be a flirty swagger. As a floating ghost, though, it was lost in translation and she sort of bobbled toward him.

"It's up to Harper, it's her book club."

I looked from Jackson's hopeful face to Whitney's pleading one. "Oh fine, you can come. Thursday at seven sharp."

His smile lit up his face and stole my breath. He really was gorgeous to look at, and I had to remind myself, again, that he was dating Liliana, his co-worker.

"Thanks, Harper. I'll be here."

He opened the door and I called after him, "You'll need to bring your own copy of the book."

"Will do." And then he was gone.

Wendy fanned herself dramatically. "Phew wee, that boy is *hawt*."

"That's your hormones talking," I chided, crossing to the coffee pot and pouring myself a cup.

"Yeah well, I'm dead. Pretty sure I don't have hormones, and I agree, he's as hot as a summer day," Whitney said, just before she vaporized into thin air.

Cradling the cup in my hands and inhaling the intoxicating aroma, I closed my eyes in bliss, soaking in a brief moment of silence before my eyes popped open and I pinned Wendy with my gaze. "Have you two talked yet?" I asked.

"Not really." A blush crept up her neck and she wrung her hands together. "But she doesn't seem angry at me and, you know, apparently, she says she knew about me and Bruce, and was planning on leaving him anyway, so..."

"Maybe you'll get the chance for a quiet word at the book club, if you're coming?" I prompted.

"Well Bruce and I were both intending to come, but now I'm not so sure it's a good idea, if Jackson is coming. Because then Whitney will definitely be there, and she hasn't seen Bruce since...you know."

"She died." I nodded. It was a strange love triangle, but if ghost Whitney was okay with it, who was I to question it. Wendy pushed herself to her feet and crossed the floor to tape a piece of paper to the front window.

"You going?" she asked, nodding at the poster she'd just put up, advertising the annual Whitefall Cove fundraiser ball.

"Sure am. I wouldn't miss it." Heaven help us all. I hadn't intended to go, hadn't *wanted* to go, but once more I'd underestimated small-town politics and sense of community—it seemed the whole town was attending and Gran wouldn't forgive me if I bailed.

"You don't look very happy about it." Wendy pointed out. She wasn't wrong.

"You know the story," I grumbled. "The last ball I went to was the one where I caught Simon cheating. That was two months ago. I'm really not in the mood for another."

Ever the optimist, Wendy beamed at me. "It will be different this time, you'll see. No stuffy professors or librarians—no offense—and everyone here knows you, loves you. It'll be great."

"This Decadent Desserts competition is new." I changed the topic.

"Oh yes, they brought that in, oh, about three years ago, I think."

"And I hear Bonnie Emerson has won all three years." Now it was my turn to grin, for I'd been listening to Gran rant about knocking Bonnie off her perch this year and taking over the coveted position of first place with her chocolate crepe cake.

Wendy rubbed her belly in appreciation. "Mmm, Bonnie's angel food cake is divine, that's for sure."

"Well, brace yourself. Gran is determined to topple her rival with her chocolate crepe cake. But keep that under your hat, I think it's a secret," I quickly added, belatedly remembering Gran had sworn me to secrecy as she practiced in the kitchen. She'd gone through several dessert recipes before deciding the chocolate crepe cake was going to be the one that wins this year.

"Is that what you're wearing?"

Turning from the mirror, I smoothed my hands down over my hips and eyed one of my best friends, Monica. "Why? What's wrong with it?"

She peered at me with her exotic blue eyes, tossing her hair over her shoulder as she reclined on my bed. I hadn't seen much of Monica since my return to Whitefall Cove, our schedules out of sync since she's a vampire and I'm a witch. Not that our species are enemies or anything, just that she's a night owl, sleeping during the day, and I keep more traditional hours.

Archie, my cat—and familiar—jumped up onto the bed and headbutted Monica for attention. Absently, she ran her hand over his orange fur, eliciting a loud purr of appreciation.

"You need"—she paused, pursing her lips—"to be showing more skin."

"You've been hanging out with Gran too much," I muttered. Gran was into exposing quite a lot of flesh. Her fashion sense was enough to make your eyes bleed, but Gran was, well, she was Gran. Unique. And I loved her to pieces, but I'd seen way too much of her eighty-year-old body than any granddaughter should have to endure. Which was also why I was moving out. The old lighthouse caretaker's cottage had become available to rent and I signed the lease last week.

"But seriously..." Turning back to the mirror, I twisted my hair and held it on top of my head with one hand, moving this way and that to capture every angle of my reflection in the strapless ruby red evening gown I'd squeezed myself into. "This is okay, right? It's been a long time since I've attended the Whitefall Cove Annual Fundraiser Ball." I ignored Monica's previous comment of showing more flesh—my arms and shoulders were bare, that was more than enough.

"It'll do, I suppose." She yawned before moving Archie from her lap and standing. "I'm getting hungry. Best I go before I get too distracted by that throat of yours."

She was gone before I could respond. As it was, my hand fluttered at my throat—I never knew how to respond to Monica's jokes about drinking blood. Would she really take a bite out of me if she let herself get too hungry? We'd grown up together, she was a born vampire, and never in all that time had I seen her succumb to bloodlust. I knew she'd adopted a purely synthetic diet, and that appeared to keep her fully functioning as a vampire, but was it enough?

After one last critical look, I released my hair and unzipped the dress. It immediately fell in a puddle at my feet and I stepped out of it, picking up the crimson fabric and securing it back on its hanger. The ball was this weekend and the only formal dress I had was back in East Dondure—and I had zero intentions of contacting my ex-fiancé, Simon, and asking him to ship it to me.

That's if he even still had it. I'd left it in a crumpled heap on the bedroom floor when I fled, just before Christmas. And here we were, days away from Valentine's Day, and I still hadn't heard a peep from him – aside from the boxes of belongings that had suddenly turned up, no note, no nothing, and the handwriting on the labels hadn't been Simon's. Maybe his girlfriend had got sick of my stuff and sent everything on. Everything except for the ballgown that is. Not that I wanted to hear from Simon. Oh no, I wanted nothing from that cheating piece of trash, but still, the lack of communication did sting, just a little. So, this dress would have to do. As it was, I'd spent a small fortune on it at The Twinkle Star Boutique.

The front door slammed and simultaneously Gran shouted up the stairs, "You home, Harper?"

"Coming!" Pulling on jeans and a sweatshirt, I hurried downstairs to see Gran trying to lead a cow through the front door. "What on earth is that?"

Gran paused from pulling on the rope around the cow's neck to look at me. "I would have thought it's perfectly obvious what it is. It's a cow, Harper."

"I know it's a cow." I rolled my eyes. "But what is it

doing here? And for god's sake, don't bring it into the house!"

"I have to." She continued to pull on the rope, but the cow mooed and held firm. Tilting my head, I considered the door's width and the cow's girth and figured the cow was right—it wasn't going to fit, no matter how much Gran tugged on the rope.

"Gran," I warned, and she had the good grace to look sheepish. As sheepish as you could in purple leggings, yellow Ugg boots, and a black-and-red plaid shirt with a white fluffy vest over the top. She stopped tugging and threw her hands up in the air in apparent defeat. "Okay, look. This here cow"—she pointed at the black-and-white bovine—"is Annie's Dalmatian, Rupert."

Clapping a hand over my mouth, I tried not to laugh. "What did you do?" I choked out.

"I need fresh milk for my recipe!" Gran exclaimed, hands waving madly, "Can't get any fresher than straight from a cow."

"But, Gran, he's not really a cow. He's a dog," I pointed out.

"Yes, well, he's temporarily a cow. I just need to milk him."

"Uh-uh, absolutely not." I wagged a finger at her. "Annie will go mental if she discovers you turned her dog into a cow!" I shook my head at her. "I'm sure milk from a carton will do just fine."

Annie Robins was the head witch of the Sisters of the Sacred Flame coven, of which Gran—and me, by default—was a member. And I very much doubted that Annie knew Gran had absconded with her pet.

"You spoil all my fun." Gran pouted, chin almost resting on her chest. I put my arm around her shoulders and gave her a squeeze. "Sorry, but you know I'm on probation with Drixworths. We've got to keep our magic squeaky clean."

"I'm so glad you've got your magic back." Gran perked up immediately, "And without needing a wand to boot. Goes to show what a powerful witch you are!"

"I wouldn't say that," I demurred, but Gran was right. I'd re-sat my witch's license exam and passed. However, my transgression in using magic to harm humans was a big one and Drixworths Academy of Witchcraft and Wizardry were keeping a close eye on me, which was why I was on probation and had to meet with the headmistress of our local branch on a weekly basis. It was Izzy who'd informed me that I was, indeed, quite powerful, that I didn't need a wand to channel my magic. That was also why they'd assigned Archie to me, to keep a dampener on my power.

"Come on, Rupert, let's get you sorted out, hmm?" Moving Gran to one side, I nudged Rupert out of the doorway and back into the garden. Closing my eyes, I visualized turning him back into a dog, whispered the spell under my breath, and *poof*, it was done. Rupert barked and jumped up with his paws on my shoulders, licking my face.

"Okay, okay. Down, boy." Grabbing his collar, I handed him to Gran. "Now take him back."

TWO

Gran returned from taking Rupert home, looking like she'd been dragged through a bramble bush backwards. Her hair stuck up on end and twigs and leaves were tangled amongst the strands, one sleeve was completely torn off her shirt, and her Uggs were scuffed and filthy.

"Now what's happened?" My concern overflowed as I raced toward her and wrapped an arm around her shoulders to help her inside. "Did Rupert turn on you?"

"That mangy dog doesn't have it in him." Gran puffed, but despite the bravado in her voice, I could see she was rattled.

"Come and sit down. I'll make you a cup of tea."

She leaned against me the entire walk to the

kitchen, something Gran never did. Whatever had happened was bad. Seating her at the table, I flicked my fingers at the kettle, setting it to boil, while a cup and saucer slowly spun through the air to settle gently on the countertop.

"Now, tell me exactly what happened." I leaned back in my chair and waited.

"I took Rupert back, as instructed." She snapped a sassy look at me before continuing, "All safe and sound, Annie didn't even miss him. Anyway, I took the long way home."

"Gran!" I admonished. "We've talked about this! You need to stop harassing Bonnie." I knew immediately what happened. Gran had deliberately taken the route past Bonnie Emerson's house. And judging by the state of her, I'd say Bonnie had been in her front garden when Gran went past.

"She started it!" Gran shook her fist. "Told me she looked forward to watching me lose the Decadent Desserts Competition. Said her angel food cake won every year and this year would be no exception."

"You should have walked away." I shook my head, rose to silence the screaming kettle, and poured Gran a cup of tea. I needed to keep my hands busy in case I gave in to the urge of throttling her.

"I started to. Then she squirted me with her garden hose!"

My eyebrows shot up into my hairline. "That wasn't very nice." Placing the cup of tea in front of Gran, I resumed my seat. "Why would she hose you down, unprovoked?"

Gran stirred her tea, despite not taking sugar, and refused to look at me. "It *was* unprovoked, wasn't it, Gran?" I knew it wasn't. Gran had all the sass and swagger of a dozen witches. She never backed down from a fight and was never shy about speaking her mind.

"I may have said she was troll bait," Gran muttered under her breath before taking a sip of tea. I bit back a smile. Gran called Bonnie troll bait, Bonnie squirted her with the hose, then—judging by Gran's appearance—a full-on brawl ensued.

"Are you hurt?" I asked, peering closely. Despite the dirt on her face and shrubbery in her hair, I couldn't see any obvious injuries.

"Just my pride." She shrugged, unrepentant.

"Did you win?" I asked next.

Gran smiled. "Probably a draw. We both used the same spell at the same time, a wind storm, and both got tossed on our asses."

Chuckling, I lay my hand over hers on the table top. "Seems the Crescent Coven and the Sisters of the Sacred Flame aren't that different after all."

The two covens had been in competition with each

other for as long as I could remember, and I think that's what bothered Gran the most. Not that it was Bonnie Emerson who was long-standing first prize holder in the Decadent Desserts Competition, but it was a member of the Crescent Coven holding that position.

"I've started a bath for you. Why don't you go on up and soak away the bruises." Snapping my fingers, I made it happen, my lips curling. Now that I had my magic back, life was so much easier.

"I shouldn't let you get away with that crack about the covens," she grumbled, pushing to her feet, "but a bath is a splendid idea, and I need to get ready for my date."

"Another one?" Gran dated...frequently. With much younger men. In fact, I think she is the town's official cougar, and biggest flirt. "Who with this time?"

Her smile lit up her face. "You'll just have to wait and see. You'll be surprised!"

To say I was surprised was the understatement of the year. Possibly century. Upon opening the front door, my mouth hung open at the sight of Detective Jackson Ward standing on the front step.

"You?" I gasped, unable to comprehend that this

man, that I secretly dreamed about, was taking my Gran out on a date!

"In the flesh." He grinned, held his arms out to the side, then let them drop. "Actually, I'm here to see your Gran." His smile disappeared and a solemn expression settled over his face.

"Oh, I know. She's spent the last two hours getting ready." Standing back, I ushered him inside, my mind a whirl. Why was he dating my Gran? What happened to Liliana? *And why was he dating my Gran?*

"She told you?" He sounded surprised, brushing past me as he stepped inside and automatically turned into the sitting room. I followed.

"Why wouldn't she?" I asked.

"Because it would make you an accessory." His frown pulled his brows together and I had the urge to smooth the lines away. Clenching my hands into fists, I resisted. He was dating my Gran. And that was, quite frankly, gross.

"An accessory to a date?" My confusion doubled.

"Wait." With hands on hips, he stood before me, the T-shirt he wore beneath his suit jacket pulling taught across his chest. "What are we talking about here?"

"Your date? With my Gran?" I heard a trace of Gran's sarcasm in my tone and bit my tongue.

He snort-laughed. "Uh yeah, no." Shaking his

head, he slowly sobered. "I'm here on official police business, Harper."

Dread filled me, freezing me to the spot. "What is it? What's happened?" Pictures flitted through my mind of Gran returning this afternoon, battered and bruised from her skirmish with Bonnie. Had there been more to it than Gran had told me? Was Bonnie hurt? Had she pressed charges?

"Bonnie Emerson was killed this afternoon," he said solemnly, his green eyes full of sorrow and concern, "and I'm here to arrest Alice Brewer for her murder."

"What?" Gran screeched from the doorway, startling us both. "I did no such thing!" She stomped forward, her sequin-covered halter top dazzling as the overhead lights caught and reflected every last sequin. On her bottom half, black leggings topped electric blue shorts. And of course, sequin-covered Uggs. She was a walking disco ball.

"Let's talk about this down at the station, Alice." Jackson stepped toward her and I moved in front, blocking him. I couldn't let him arrest my Gran. The idea of her murdering Bonnie was preposterous. He sighed, shaking his head at me. "I have to do this, Harper. I'm sorry."

"It's okay, lass." Gran touched her hand to my back. "I'll go. We'll sort this out and then Jackson can spend the next decade making it up to me. I've got several ideas already."

"Gran, this is serious." I turned my head, speaking to her over my shoulder, unwilling to move and let Jackson take her away. I knew what it was like to be a suspect in a murder, and I wasn't about to let my Gran go through that. But the worst part, the part that was niggling away and burrowing deep inside, was that Jackson said he was here to arrest her. Not question her. Not interview her. *Arrest* her. Which meant the police were pretty damned sure that my Gran, Alice Brewer, killed Bonnie Emerson.

Placing one of his big hands on my shoulder, Jackson stepped close, his scent filling my nose, the warmth of his hand seeping into me, calming, but wakening emotions better left alone. He lowered his head, his face level with mine, his green eyes blazing. "Trust me on this, Harper."

I lost myself in the emerald pools of his eyes, drowning in their depths, and I vaguely wondered if he had any abilities other than being able to talk to the dead, because right now, I felt as if I were under a spell. A deep, dark, seductively delicious spell. We'd become friends, of sorts, over the last couple of months, and I told myself for the millionth time that was all it could ever be.

"You can't lock her up." My voice was barely a whisper and I had to blink away the moisture rapidly building in my eyes. I couldn't bear for Gran to be in jail. It wasn't right. "Please don't do this."

My pleading sounded pathetic to my own ears, but I couldn't stop myself.

"I have a warrant," he said flatly. "She's wanted for murder. I have to take her in." His face settled into hard lines, and just like that, he was in full-on cop mode. "Stand aside."

He didn't physically move me, but I felt his fingers tense where they rested on my shoulder. Ready to toss me aside should I prove to be a problem? I jerked away, breaking contact and whirling to face Gran, a feeling of panic sweeping over me. This couldn't be happening.

"Gran!" I cried and she cupped my face in her hands.

"It's okay, child, just breathe. And call your parents. I'm going to need a lawyer and your dad has contacts."

She kissed the tip of my nose and released me, then addressed Jackson over my shoulder. "Let's go, Detective."

I stood frozen to the spot as Jackson stepped around me, and before I could so much as suck in a breath, Gran's hands were cuffed behind her back, and Jackson was giving the right-to-remain-silent speech.

"I see you've heard I like handcuff play," Gran observed, giving him a cheeky wink. Jackson actually blushed and I stared—partly in horror, partly in disbelief. Gran was being arrested and here she was, flirting with the sexy-as-hell cop who was intent on locking her away.

"Gran." I didn't know what to say. I felt the weight of Jackson's gaze but refused to meet his eyes, instead keeping my own glued to Gran. How could he do this? Gran wasn't a murderer! My respect for him plummeted and I'm not sure what hurt more, Gran's arrest or the actions of a man I considered a friend.

The door clicked shut behind them, as soft as a whisper yet as loud as thunder in its finality. A lump knotted in my throat, and I balled my fists at my sides. I rushed to the window and peered outside, watching as Jackson assisted Gran into the back seat of his car. He shut the door gently then turned to look at the house. I quickly dropped the curtain and stepped back from the window, not wanting to be caught spying. Not that it was spying, technically. Watching. Yes, watching was a better word. But it didn't matter what I called it, I didn't want Jackson to know I was doing it.

My stomach churned and I felt sick. This couldn't be happening. Gathering my wits, I ran down the hallway back to the kitchen. I dug through my handbag for my phone and with trembling fingers, I dialed.

"Mom?" My voice broke when the call connected.

"Harper, love, what's wrong?" Her voice was so clear she could have been standing next to me, but I knew she was thousands of miles away, on the other side of the world in Australia.

"Gran's been arrested!"

"Oh God, I knew it was only a matter of time." Mom sighed. "What for? Public nudity? Drunk and disorderly?"

"Murder." There was such absolute silence I thought the line had dropped out. "Mom? You still there?"

There was a rustling, then, "Harper? It's Dad. What's happened?"

"Gran's been arrested for murder. She said to call. That you knew a good lawyer."

"What happened?" I could picture him in my mind, always calm in a crisis. I realized it had to be the middle of the night there, that I'd woken them. No wonder Mom had almost fainted. Imagine waking from your sleep to be told your mother had been arrested for murder?

"I don't know the details. Just that Bonnie Emerson was killed this afternoon and the police think Gran did it."

"Okay, love, don't panic. I'm going to call a lawyer in East Dondure, a friend of mine. He'll be in touch. He's the best, you can trust him. I'll get your mom and I on the next available flight. We'll sort this out, okay?"

My chin wobbled and a tear trickled down my cheek. "Thanks, Dad. I miss you." I hadn't realized just how much until hearing their voices. They hadn't made it home for Christmas, the archeological dig in Australia had kept them there. But now, hearing his deep voice in my ear, I longed to feel his strong arms around me, patting me between the shoulder blades like he had when I was a child, assuring me everything would be okay.

"I miss you too, sugar. We'll see you soon."

A rchie meowed, curling himself around my legs. I scooped him up, burying my face in his fur.

"I can't believe Gran killed her," I said. "Not intentionally." I added, for there was no denying Gran had returned home this afternoon frazzled and dazed after her run-in with Bonnie. Archie meowed again, bumping his nose to my chin and snuggling against me. "What do I do, Archie?" I whispered. "Wait for Mom and Dad? That'll be hours, possibly days, away."

Archie wriggled in my arms and I let him go, watching as he gracefully landed on all fours before he began to groom himself, paying particular attention to a patch of damp fur on his side where I'd buried my face. Damn it, I'd gotten snot all over my cat. Then it hit me. Why was I standing here doing nothing when I should be doing something to clear Gran's name.

"Oh my god, you're right!" I said out loud. Snatching up my bag and keys, I hurried for the front door, Archie's paws sliding on the wooden floor as he hurried after me.

I was pulling away, Archie perched beside me on the passenger seat, when another car pulled up outside. A glance in the rearview mirror showed a man, dressed in a suit, heading up the garden path. Gran's date, I presumed, and I felt sorry for the guy who'd effectively been stood up. I wondered who he was, and was incredibly grateful Gran wasn't dating Jackson. Then my mind replayed this evening's events and my mood switched to one of anger. How could he believe Gran was capable of murder? My jaw ached from clenching my teeth so tight.

There was only one thing to do. Prove her innocence myself. Which was why I found myself checking out Bonnie Emerson's house. Or, to be more precise, breaking into Bonnie Emerson's house. Considering the events that had occurred this evening, I felt justified in my actions. I kept telling myself that when I crept around the side of the whiteboard house to the back door. Police tape crossed the front door, so I'd vetoed it, deciding instead to try the rear of the house. Plus, I had less chance of being seen.

To my utmost surprise, the back door was unlocked, and I paused as the knob clicked beneath my hand. *Probably should have worn gloves,* I realized, two seconds too late. Sucking in a breath, I glanced around before easing the door open and sliding inside. The door opened directly into Bonnie's kitchen. I don't know what I'd been expecting, but it wasn't this. A chair was pulled out from the table, loose rope pooled around the legs, and the floor around the chair was littered with cake crumbs. Not so much crumbs. Chunks. She died here. In that chair.

I'd never asked how she'd died and now I wish I had before blundering into her kitchen. Someone had tied her to the chair, that was the only explanation for the rope. The cake was puzzling though. Maybe it had been dropped in the struggle, for there had to have been a struggle to get her into the chair in the first place. Circling the table, I did my best not to tread on any of the cake. There was no blood—so she hadn't been stabbed. Strangled maybe? There was a lot of rope. More than necessary, in my opinion. Yards of the stuff. Or suffocated? I couldn't see anything laying around, like a plastic bag, but of course, the police would have taken it as evidence.

On the table was a bowl of eggs, complete with feathers and smeared chicken poop. Fresh. Home laid. The bowl was full to brimming. A container with the word "flour" on the label stood next to a mixing bowl, along with a wooden spoon. She had either been baking or getting ready to bake. Which made sense given the Decadent Desserts competition was mere days away.

Covering everything was fingerprint powder. I was wasting my time, I'd find nothing here that the police hadn't already found. And if I wanted to know what they'd already found, I'd have to talk to Jackson, and hope to god he'd tell me. That's if I decided I was even speaking to him.

Archie wove between my ankles, meowed once, and then headed into the living room. Nothing to see here. Archie must have thought the same because he explored every room downstairs before heading upstairs, and I decided to follow.

It wasn't until I stuck my head into the attic that I found anything of interest. This was where Bonnie practiced magic. Not only could I feel the remnants of it, but I could see her altar, a dark purple cloth draped over a dresser, candles, chalice, and mortar and pestle. Her magic was strong—even though she was no longer on this mortal realm, her magic lived on and it pulled and repulsed me at the same time. Shivers danced over my skin as I took a step inside. The floorboard creaked underfoot, unnerving in its loudness. Hesitantly, I crossed the room to the altar, standing where she would have stood countless times before, and looked up and out the round window directly in front of me.

"You're here, aren't you?" I said. No reply. Looking over my shoulder, I'd half-expected to see the ghost of Bonnie Emerson behind me. But she wasn't there. Peering into the dim corners of the attic, I waited. She didn't materialize, but I swear I could feel her.

"Jesus, Harper," I muttered to myself. "You're freaking yourself out." I looked down at the altar and that's when I noticed it. She'd burned something in the mortar and pestle. I reached in and pulled out a piece of paper, singed around the edges, but parts still legible.

"What were you putting behind you, Bonnie?" Burning was symbolic. Letting go, releasing whatever it was into the past and moving forward. Only what was it?

Holding up the paper, I squinted at it. Neat cursive handwriting, and the paper had been scorched in places, but I made out some words—*my darling, your beautiful eyes, love.* I had to assume what I was holding was a love letter. The amount of ashes in the pestle indicated more than one letter had been burnt.

"Who was your boyfriend, Bonnie?" I asked out loud, "and why were you burning his letters?"

"What are you doing here?"

I let out a shriek and spun to face the door, relaxing a little when I saw it was Jackson.

"I don't think I should answer that," I replied, doing my best to look like I just hadn't been busted breaking into someone's house. "What are *you* doing here?"

"Investigating a murder." His eyes narrowed on the piece of paper pinched between my thumb and forefinger.

"Too bad you didn't do more investigating before arresting Gran," I snapped. "Then you might have found this." I held it out and he stepped forward but instead of taking it from me, he peered at it while reaching into his pocket for an evidence bag.

"Love letter?" he asked.

"I'd say so. I didn't know Bonnie was seeing anyone." I watched as he sealed the plastic bag and tucked it carefully inside his jacket pocket.

"Nor did I. No one mentioned anything."

"Who found her?"

"Kristen Lane. Know her?"

I shrugged. "Sort of. She's younger than me. And a member of the Crescent Coven. In fact, her grandmother, Delores Lane, is next in line to be head witch."

"Is that right?" A dark brow arched over impossibly green eyes and I bit my lip.

"I'm sure she told you all of that herself." I huffed,

feeling suddenly uncomfortable in this small space with him. It was so unfair my hormones went into overdrive around him and it was totally unreciprocated. Not to mention, I was pissed at him for what he'd done.

He inclined his head. "She did. She dropped by to pick Bonnie up, they were having some sort of Coven... meeting?" He fished for the right word.

"Probably a ceremony," I supplied. "We're having one tomorrow night. To bless the Decadent Desserts entry."

His eyebrows shot into his hairline. "For real?"

Crossing my arms over my chest, I shot him a look. "For real. A blessing ceremony."

"What's that entail?" With his head cocked to one side, he looked like a curious puppy. My irritation rose.

"None of your business, *Detective*." Brushing past him, I hurried back down the stairs to the ground floor, stopping when I reached the crime scene in the kitchen. I felt his warmth when he came up behind me.

"How did she die?" I whispered.

"I could say it's none of your business," he drawled, and I stiffened as he continued, "but I won't. She choked. Large amounts of cake were shoved into her mouth, blocking her airway."

"Oh my god. That's the cake? On the floor?" I pointed with a shaking hand.

"And the cake? Was it her angel food cake? Her entry for the Decadent Desserts competition?" Because if it was, that was very symbolic. No wonder he thought Gran did it. Not only was Gran arguing with Bonnie, but she was in direct competition with her for the title of Decadent Dessert winner.

"We believe so. Waiting on forensics."

I nodded while studying the table and its contents, pushing aside the horror of Bonnie's death and how awful it would have been to die like that.

"Did you see her? Upstairs?" I asked as I looked over at him, remembering the feeling I'd had in the attic.

Jackson shook his head. "Not exactly."

"What does that mean?"

He lifted one shoulder in a shrug. "It means that who I saw may or may not have been Bonnie. There was an orb, shapeless, hovering in the attic."

"An orb? So...not a ghost?"

"Sometimes the afterlife leaves behind a lot of their energy and it doesn't fully dissipate, so it remains as an orb, a sentient—usually—ball of power."

"Sentient. So, it doesn't move? Do anything? Do they go away eventually?" I'd never heard of this phenomenon before and was curious.

"There are no hard and fast rules," Jackson explained, "I haven't seen them move, not in a way that indicates they're trying to communicate."

I was thinking about the orb Jackson had seen in the attic and the feeling that I'd had, that Bonnie's spirit was there, when I had a realization. "I knew something was missing!" I practically shouted, spinning on my heel and hurrying back up the stairs. I passed Archie on the staircase, his fur rising as I rushed past him.

"Wait! What?" Jackson called out, his feet thundering on the staircase behind me.

"Bonnie's grimoire. It's not on her altar." Flinging open the attic door, I hurried to the altar, scanning the surface. All her tools for witchcraft were here, but no grimoire.

"Grimoire?" Jackson asked, joining me.

"Spell book," I explained. "We each have our own book where we write our spells and notes and things. Usually they are something that's handed down through generations. They are very precious."

"Valuable?"

"Not in the monetary sense. But to the magic world, yes, very valuable. I'd even say that aside from her wand, her grimoire is a witch's most treasured possession."

Jackson rubbed his chin, his fingers dragging across the stubble with a rasping noise, loud in the attic.

"Maybe she kept it someplace else? Locked away for safe keeping?" he suggested.

I considered what he'd said. It was possible, I suppose, that Bonnie had hidden her grimoire but that raised the question of why. She lived alone. Who was she hiding it from?

"Doubtful," I finally said, "but it wouldn't hurt to look."

"Here." Jackson tossed me a pair of latex gloves. "I'll search in here, you take Bonnie's bedroom."

Snapping on the gloves, I left Jackson in the attic, rummaging among boxes stacked at one end, while I headed to Bonnie's bedroom upstairs. Turning the door knob and pushing the door open, I stood on the threshold for a moment, breathing in her scent, which hit me in the face as soon as I'd opened the door. I crossed to the dresser and picked up the bottle of lavender perfume, bringing it to my nose, breathing it in and closing my eyes. I couldn't sense her here like I had in the attic, but I had the feeling that Bonnie Emerson wasn't gone, not completely.

Putting down the perfume bottle, I got to work. I'd considered using a summoning spell, but I had no connection to Bonnie's grimoire, it would be drenched in the other woman's magic and essence, potentially blocking any magic I used to locate it. I made a mental note to ask Gran if it was possible to track the grimoire if we didn't find it today.

I was feeling through a pile of sweaters in the

dresser when a floorboard creaked in the hallway outside.

"Finished already?" I said to Jackson.

"Still playing detective, Ms. Jones?" Officer Lilliana Miles asked. I froze, then peeked over my shoulder. She stood in the doorway, her navy-blue uniform immaculate, hands on hips, face cold.

"Hi," I offered, not quite sure what I should say.

Jackson must have heard us because I heard his boots on the attic steps. Lilliana did too, for she crossed her arms over her chest and waited. Not impatiently, not exactly, but more...resigned. As if she'd known we were here together.

"Who authorized this?" she demanded once Jackson was within earshot.

"You know I'm involved in this case," I said before Jackson could respond. Lilliana shot me a look, one that said I should shut my mouth and not say another word. Considering she was the one in uniform, sporting a gun, I opted to do just that.

"Just hold on a minute." Jackson brushed past her and stood between Lilliana and me, as if he expected us to launch into some sort of catfight at any moment. I cocked my head, wondering why he thought that. I had no intentions of brawling with his girlfriend. And just who was he protecting in this scenario? Her? Or me?

"She's helping me look for evidence." Jackson kept

his back to me, blocking my view of Lilliana. "Why are you here?"

"Preliminary autopsy results are in."

"You could have called that in." He seemed irritated, his voice tight. "But since you're here now, you may as well tell me."

"In front of her?"

He inclined his head. "In front of her."

"Cause of death was asphyxia as a result of choking. Upper lip lacerations, hematomas to the head, neck, and chest. Contusions to both arms and wrists."

Jackson nodded. "Consistent with being tied to a chair and force-fed. Thank you, Officer Miles, that will be all."

Despite not being able to see their exchange, I could feel it. There was animosity in spades, so much that I rolled my shoulders to shrug off the tension settling there. Lilliana stepped sideways and eyeballed me, her next words directed at me.

"Do me a favor? Try not to come around here again." Then she was gone, her footsteps retreating down the hallway, down the stairs. A door slammed, then I heard the sound of a car door closing and an engine revving.

"She doesn't appear to like me very much." I sounded pitiful even to myself, which hadn't been my intention.

"She doesn't like anyone very much," Jackson said gruffly, then changed the subject. "How's it going in here? Find anything?"

"Not yet. I don't think it's here. I can feel a sense of her, of Bonnie, but not her magic. If the grimoire is anywhere, I'd say it's in the attic."

"I've got an idea," I said.

"Is it a good one?" Jackson asked, looking down at me.

"Ha. Ha," I grumbled. "We already know that we have some sort of mysterious mystical connection to the otherworld, that when we are together, the ghost of Whitney Sims appears. I'd like to try and channel our power, see if we can reach Bonnie."

"Can't hurt to try"—he nodded, leading the way back up the stairs to the attic—"but remember, it didn't happen straight away with Whitney."

"I remember. You said you saw an orb in the attic. And the attic is where I feel her magic. If she's still here, that's where she'll be. And if we can communicate with her..." I trailed off.

"She can tell us what happened. Who killed her," Jackson supplied.

"Exactly."

Standing side-by-side in the attic, a shiver danced over my skin, causing goose bumps. I was still weirded out by ghosts.

"Have you always been a necromancer?" I asked, wondering what it had been like for Jackson growing up. Had he had an invisible friend who was really a ghost?

"Yes."

"Was it hard? Seeing what other people couldn't? Did they think you were crazy?"

He glanced at me, then shrugged. "Not really. My grandmother had the gift. She saw me talking with the ghost of our neighbor when I was a toddler and guided me through it. There were times, as a kid, that I didn't immediately realize that the person I was talking to was departed. That's when it got problematic."

"Yet you decided to join the police force?"

"I use my gift on the force. Just because I talk to dead people doesn't mean I need to set up shop as a psychic or some such thing. I don't draw attention to it —most people don't know—but I'd rather help them by solving their..." he paused, and the penny finally dropped.

"Oh! You use your gift to solve their murders! To bring them justice." I felt embarrassed I hadn't figured that out earlier. He must think I'm an absolute idiot, although he didn't let on, just lifted one shoulder and continued speaking.

"It seemed the right thing to do. Most of the ghosts I see are here because they died violently and unexpectedly. Not always a crime, sometimes due to an accident, in which case I try and help them come to terms with their passing."

"Is it true that they remain on this realm due to unfinished business?"

"Sometimes. Not always. Some can't bear to leave, they'd rather remain with their family, unheard and unseen, than move on."

"But you help them move on? When they're ready?"

He shrugged again. "I do my best."

"Whitney didn't move on. Even when we solved her murder," I pointed out.

"Because she didn't want to. It's a choice. For some, it's a no-brainer. They see the light, they cross over. Others see the light and decide to stay."

"Do they see the light again? Like, do they get a second opportunity to cross over?" I'd never talked about this stuff with anyone before and found it fascinating.

"Again, sometimes. There are no hard and fast rules. Every situation is different." He held up his hand to silence me, his eyes intent on something across the attic. I turned to look and saw a very faint glow.

"Is that it?" I whispered. "Is that the orb you saw?"

"Yes," he whispered back. "Can you see it?"

"I see a very dull glow, barely there."

"It's bright for me. About four feet tall." He reached down and entwined his fingers with mine, our palms pressed together. I did my best to ignore the spark of electricity that shot up my arm at the intimate contact. "Concentrate," he ordered.

I squeezed my eyes shut and tried to do as instructed, focusing my energy on the orb.

"It's working," he whispered, and I cracked open my eyes to see the orb, much brighter than it had been before.

"It's bigger. Brighter," I said. "Has it changed for you? Is she taking shape? Is it Bonnie?"

"No," he said, voice low, a hint of puzzlement in his tone, "but it's changing color and moving."

He was right, the orb was turning and moving closer to us. Could it sense us? See us? Suddenly, it flared, the light so bright it hurt my eyes and I flung my arm over my face.

"Get down!" Jackson shouted, then tackled me to the floor, his body hard and heavy on top of mine as he shielded me from the orb, which flew over us and disappeared with a loud *pop*.

"What happened?" I grunted, pushing at him. He

planted his palms on the floor by the side of my head and levered himself up, easing the pressure on my lungs.

"I think it got angry. I don't think it's a ghost at all. Energy, yes, but not a spirit." With his face this close to mine, I could see the flecks of gold in his green eyes and the dimple in his cheek where his mouth quirked into a smile. Then he was moving away, standing over me and holding his hand down to help me up.

"I didn't hurt you, did I?" he asked, eyes running over my body. I dusted off my jeans and shook my head. "I'm fine. You took me by surprise is all." I looked around the attic—the orb had gone and all that remained was the remnants of Bonnie's magic.

"I can still feel Bonnie's magic but not the energy of that thing. How about you?" I asked.

Jackson shook his head. "I see nothing. Bonnie isn't here. She's crossed over." He sounded sure of that and I couldn't help the disappointment that we wouldn't get to talk to her, to find out who killed her and clear Gran's name.

"So that begs the question, what the hell was that?" I waved my hand to where the orb had been hovering.

"I have no idea"—Jackson ran a hand around the back of his neck—"but I've got a real bad feeling."

Goose bumps broke out over my skin as a shiver

ran up my spine. This was dark. Was someone using black magic?

Jackson walked me to my car, carrying Archie the entire way. I'd parked two blocks away to avoid the neighbors noticing me snooping. I waited for a lecture from him on sticking my nose into police business and basically telling me to stay out of it, but he didn't, and that confused me more than ever. I'd been so angry with him yet working together had made my anger disappear. But now I was alone, and my unruly emotions resurfaced. I was angry, upset, and afraid. Afraid for Gran and what might happen to her. Angry with Jackson for arresting her. And upset with myself for still harboring unrequited feelings for him.

Pulling up outside Gran's house and parking, I waited for Archie to jump out of the car and down the garden path ahead of me. Once inside, it hit me. An avalanche of emotion. I picked up a lamp from the hallway table and threw it, tears welling in my eyes when it hit the floor with a satisfying crash.

A loud thumping on the front door scared me to death. With a high-pitched "Eeek!" I spun, facing the door, hand to my chest.

"Hello? Everything okay in there?" A man's voice. A strange man's voice. Could this be Gran's date? Had he hung around all this time, waiting for one of us to return? I wasn't sure if that was dedication or desperation.

Cracking open the door, I peered through the slit.

"Yes?" Standing on my doorstep was a bad guy, I was sure of it. He had that vibe. He was tall, with a solid frame and dark hair, so dark it looked black in this light. In denim jeans, a black T-shirt, and bomber jacket, he looked like he worked out. A lot.

"Harper Jones?" This guy screamed *danger* in neon letters. It was in the hard set of his jaw, the steadiness of his dark eyes as they swept over me, the scar cutting through his right eyebrow that had me wondering just how he'd got it. A knife fight? He looked the type.

"Well?"

Well what? Oh, right. "Yes?" I squeaked, my voice rising three octaves. Now I sounded like a chipmunk. I cleared my throat and tried again. "Yes. I'm Harper Jones. Who are you?"

"Blake Tennant." His hand disappeared into his jacket pocket and I had visions of him pulling a gun. A possible overreaction, but nonetheless, he looked the type. I sagged in relief when, instead of pulling out a weapon, he handed me a business card. I squinted down at it, then looked up at him in disbelief.

"You're a lawyer?"

He inclined his head, his gaze never leaving mine.

"Where's your suit?" I blurted.

"At the dry cleaners," he replied, unfazed, a slow, wolfish smile sliding across his face. "Are you going to invite me in?"

Was I? An excellent question as I stood hesitantly clutching the door, my heart pounding in my chest. Dad had said he had a lawyer friend, but this man didn't look like your typical lawyer. Seemed he'd gotten tired of my hesitation because he slowly raised his hand and gave the door a push. I let it slide from my fingers, revealing the shattered lamp strewn down the hallway.

"You okay?" he asked, observing the destruction before turning his impossibly dark gaze to my face. He smirked, his eyes taking in my jeans, sweater, and booted feet. He leaned forward and flicked something from my shoulder, and I jerked back.

"You had a piece of lamp," he said, his eyes gleaming.

I felt heat crawl up my neck and into my face and knew my cheeks were reflecting my embarrassment with a red glow. Busted having a tantrum and throwing a lamp, covering myself and everything else in shards of glass. *Smart, Harper, real smart.*

"Are you going to invite me in?" he repeated, leaning casually against the door frame, waiting.

"Nuh-uh." I shook my head.

He grinned. A slow, wicked grin that reached all the way to his dark eyes. It was the kind of grin that made women either cower in fear or want to rip his clothes off. I wasn't one hundred percent sure what camp I fell into.

"Okay," he said, cocking his head to one side, "how about we talk out here? I'm sure the neighbors are keen to listen in on what we have to discuss."

"Oh?" I licked my lips, my mouth dry.

"Alice Brewer." He raised one eyebrow at me.

"Come in." I turned away, my boots crunching on broken glass. The door closed quietly, and his boots crunched glass behind me.

"Got something to clean that up with?" he asked.

"No need." I stood in the center of the living room and waved my hand. The lamp put itself back together in reverse slow motion, all the minute particles of crushed and broken glass and ceramic repositioning themselves until the lamp was whole once more and sitting on the hallway table.

He nodded. "Impressive."

"Thanks."

He looked me up and down, his eyes doing a slow, thorough appraisal. "Do I make you nervous?"

I nodded, which, of course, caused his smile to grow into a full-fledged grin, complete with wolfish white teeth. "Good."

He had me on the defensive, and I didn't like it. I didn't know what to think, of him, of my rioting emotions.

"About my Gran—" My chipmunk voice was back, and I cleared my throat again. "About Gran," I repeated. "You can get her off?"

"Get her off?" The sexual innuendo was clear, and I felt myself blush. If my cheeks got any hotter, I'd erupt.

"Out of jail. Clear her name?" I snapped, annoyed at him, and at my reaction to him. He was way too good-looking for his own good and the animal magnetism pouring from him was off the charts. He was older than me, in his late thirties, maybe early forties, which told me he was the type of man who knew what he wanted. That he also knew what a woman wanted—and exactly how to provide it. I gulped.

He must have decided he was done toying with me because he eased himself into an armchair and indicated I should do the same. I did, simply because I was unsure how much longer my legs would hold me up.

"The evidence against Alice is circumstantial. Not really enough for an arrest warrant but they got a judge to sign off on it, so not much we can do about that now," he said. "Our first priority is setting bail."

"Bail?" I repeated.

"A sum of money that's lodged to guarantee she appears in court."

I blushed again, feeling like an idiot. I knew what

bail was, but for some reason, around him I was reduced to one-word sentences. He must think I'm an absolute ditz.

"I know what bail is," I grumbled, crossing my arms over my chest.

He grinned. "Okay then."

"I'm not an idiot," I continued, secretly appalled at how off-balance I was around him.

His smile widened, a dimple punctuating his left cheek. Clearly, he was enjoying this.

"I never thought for one minute that you were."

He reached into his pocket and pulled out his phone. "Mind if I record this?"

"Record what?" I wanted to reassure him I wasn't really this stupid in real life, but I was having issues following our conversation.

"Our interview. I want you to tell me everything that happened." He glanced up from his phone and saw my confusion. His face softened. "I know it's late. You're tired, I get it. But I need to gather as many witness statements as I can. The sooner I can get Alice's bail application in, the quicker we get her out of jail."

I nodded. Made perfect sense.

"Take it from the top. There was an altercation this afternoon between the victim and Alice, yes? Tell me about that."

I leaned forward in my chair and told him about

Gran and Bonnie's argument that afternoon, how Gran had been taking Annie's dog back—leaving out the part about Gran turning the dog into a cow—but he was good. He knew something was missing and he leaned forward, eyes intent.

"Stop." His brows pulled together in concentration. "Something happened. Something else happened that you're not telling me."

I looked away, toward the fireplace, stalling.

"Harper." His long fingers wrapped around my wrist, drawing my attention back to him. "I'm *very* good at what I do. But I can't help you if you don't tell me the *entire* story."

I looked into his dark eyes, transfixed, almost hypnotized as his thumb rubbed the inside of my wrist.

"Tell me," he demanded, his voice low and quiet. And I did. I told him the whole sorry sordid tale, and that despite Gran being in the wrong, she wouldn't have—couldn't have—killed Bonnie.

An hour later, he tucked his phone back into his jacket pocket and stretched the kinks out of his shoulders.

"Meet me at the police station at nine," he said, as he stood and headed for the door. Was that it? It felt so...anticlimactic.

"Okay."

He must have heard something in my voice

because he turned, those dark eyes flashing, a sinful smirk curling his lips. "Sweet dreams."

Before I could react, he was gone. Sweet dreams? *Sweet dreams!* How could I even contemplate sleeping while Gran was in jail? My eyes welled again, thinking of her in a cell, on a hard cot with nothing but a scratchy blanket for comfort.

Archie appeared, jumping onto my lap and biscuiting my legs into submission. I didn't have the energy to move, slumping back to give him more room. I rested my head against the back of the armchair and mulled over the events of the day. At some point, I fell asleep, where I did indeed have sweet dreams. Of one sexy lawyer named Blake Tennant.

Oh boy.

I woke up the following morning with the sun blazing in my face and a crick in my neck. I was still in the armchair where I'd fallen asleep, but Archie had long since left. Reaching forward with a groan and a creaking of bones, I picked up my phone from the coffee table and glanced at the time. Eight forty-five. Holy heck, I had told Blake I'd meet him at the station at nine. Staggering to my feet, I stumbled down the hallway to use the bathroom, smoothed the wrinkles from my clothes as best as I could, and cast a longing glance at the shower. *Later*, I promised myself.

I arrived at the Police Station at eight fifty-eight a.m. Blake was already there, filling out what appeared to be a mountain of paperwork.

"Oh good, you made it," he said, without turning. How did he do that? How did he know it was me?

"I said I would." My voice came out like a bucket of rusty nails and his head swiveled just as Officer Miles appeared behind the counter. Oh goody. Her eyes ran over me from head to toe and then she smirked—the kind of smirk that told me I had toilet paper stuck to my shoe or something equally mortifying. Before I could react, Jackson joined her and his eyes widened at the sight of me. *What the hell?*

My confused expression must have betrayed me because Blake put down the pen and turned to fully face me.

"Come here."

I shouldn't have listened, should definitely not have obeyed, but in my caffeine-deprived brain, resistance was useless, and I stepped toward him, stopping just short of touching. He raised his hand and ran it from the top of my head down the length of my hair, smiling slightly as he did so. Then I got it. Bedhead. I hadn't stopped to look in a mirror, no doubt my hair had been in a massive beehive around my head—that was my default setting each and every morning.

"Thanks," I said gruffly, stepping back and putting some space between us.

"Anytime. Anytime at all." That wolfish grin was back, and my heart skipped a beat. Then Jackson caught my attention or, more precisely, the dark scowl on his face. Now what? Had he and Liliana had words again? I couldn't sense as much tension between them this morning, but that was most likely due to the overwhelming presence of Blake Tennant and the effect he had on my senses.

Blake turned back to the counter and pushed the paperwork toward Jackson.

"Signed, sealed, and delivered."

"Officer Miles, would you bring Mrs. Brewer through, please?" Jackson initialed the paperwork while Liliana spun on her heel without replying and disappeared down the corridor. "Take a seat," Jackson said curtly. I frowned at him. What's up his butt?

Blake cupped my elbow and guided me toward the chairs lining one wall. I sank down, my head fuzzy. I really needed a caffeine hit—I couldn't think straight, I felt as if I were sleepwalking.

"Rough night?" Blake asked, taking the seat next to me, the length of his denim-clad thigh heating mine where it touched.

"Slept in the chair," I grumbled, frowning when he chuckled. It wasn't funny. None of this was funny.

"Hey." He wrapped one big hand over mine where it rested on my knee and I marveled at the contrast in our skin tone, his tanned to a smooth mocha, mine as pale as snow. "Everything's going to be okay." He mistook my sleep-deprived, caffeine-deprived, state for concern over Gran.

"Thank you for everything you've done." I forced a

smile. It was my turn to reassure him. And I was grateful. If he hadn't turned up, Gran would still be rotting in a cell.

"I knew it." He studied my face, his eyes intent, his own lips soft and curling slightly at the corners.

"What?" He was so confusing I couldn't keep up.

"That your smile would transform you."

Oh. Said smile slipped. I didn't know what to make of his words. Was he coming on to me? Was that ethical? But technically, his client was Gran, not me, so did that mean...but what about Jackson? My eyes shot to the man in question, watching us with a scowl on his face from behind the counter. For months, I'd fantasized over him, out of reach because he was with another woman. Could I have switched affection so quickly, so easily? It made me uncomfortable to think I could. I wasn't even sure that was what was going on here.

Blake chuckled. "Your face is an open book," he said. "You might want to work on that."

Before I could reply, Gran waltzed around the corner, a massive smile on her face.

"Oh hi, Jackson." She beamed at him. "Thanks for a wonderful night." She punctuated her words with a wink. "Sorry to take him away from you, darl," she added to Liliana, who stood with her arms crossed and her mouth pulled together in the perfect imitation of a cat's rear end. I giggled. She glared at me, her mouth puckering even tighter, if that was possible, and I bit the inside of my cheek to keep from laughing out loud.

Gran was still in her party gear from the night before, the sequins catching the fluorescent lights and sending patterns dancing across the walls and floor.

"And you must be my knight in shining armor." She sashayed up to Blake who'd stood at her arrival, wrapped her arms around his waist, and hugged him. Tightly. "Thank you."

"My pleasure, ma'am," he drawled, not in the least bit uncomfortable with the eighty-year-old sex bomb plastered to his front and her hand sneaking down to cup one cheek and squeeze. She turned her head and grinned at me. "He works out," she told me. "Buns of steel."

Oh god. My cheeks burned but Blake took it in stride, disengaging himself from her but keeping a hand at her back. "Need your signature on a few things, Alice, then we can blow this joint."

"Promises, promises," she declared dramatically but went with him to the counter where Liliana was pushing a sheet of paper and pen toward them.

"Harper." Jackson had rounded the counter and was now easing himself into the seat Blake had just vacated.

"What?" Okay, I was unreasonably surly without my morning coffee. He should know this by now and cut me some slack.

"I had to do it. There was a warrant."

I lifted one shoulder. So there was a warrant, so what?

"You'd rather someone else do it. You rather Liliana?" he pressed, and I snapped my head round to look at him so fast I feared whiplash.

"You. Arrested. My. Gran." My voice was soft and calm and deadly. He swallowed, leaning back, away from me. I felt a little thrill of power.

"I let you help me with the investigation, didn't I?"

Damn it, he was being reasonable. Yes. He'd let me poke around Bonnie's house last night and had helped me try and contact her. That didn't mean I wasn't still mad at him.

Gran and Blake had finished at the counter and Gran came bouncing over—I assumed they'd provided her with coffee in her cell. That was the only explanation I could come up with for her perky early morning mood.

"Thanks for a great night, handsome." She planted a kiss on Jackson's cheek and again, he blushed, tipping his head at her.

"Take care," he said gruffly, disengaging from her and hurrying away without a backward glance, leaving me more confused than ever.

"Jesus." Gran stood with her hands on her hips and examined me. "You look like shit. Let's go get breakfast."

We sat in Bean Me Up. I hadn't expected Blake to join us, but he'd followed me and Gran in his rental car and was now ensconced at our cozy window table.

"You move fast," Gran told him, studying him intently as he stirred sugar into his coffee.

He shrugged. "It's what I do."

"She's got a point," I said. "Dad called you last night and you were here, what, an hour or two later? It's at least a four-hour drive from East Dondure."

"Who said I drove?" Of course. I wanted to smack my forehead on the table. He must have flown in, although it would have had to have been a charter flight. No commercials flights were available after sundown in Whitefall Cove.

"Open book," he said under his breath, his eyes twinkling. "That your store?" He nodded toward The Dusty Attic, directly across the road from where we were sitting.

I smiled softly, looking at my bookstore through the window. "It is."

"Wendy open up for you today?" Gran asked, bringing my attention back to her.

I nodded again. "Yeah. I wasn't sure how long all this would take, or where we go from here, so Wendy is holding down the fort for now." Which reminded me. "So what happens now?" I directed the question to Blake.

"Now you go about your business. You"—he inclined his head at Gran—"stay out of trouble. And don't leave town. And you"—this time, his head came my way—"no more amateur detective work. Leave this to the professionals."

"Hey!" I protested. "I'm no amateur. I solved Whitney Sims' murder."

"That does not make you a detective. Look at it this way. We are all agreed that your Gran didn't kill Bonnie Emerson, right?" We nodded. "Which means the murderer is still out there. Knocking off witches. You two are witches, and you, Harper, have a habit of sticking your nose in where it doesn't belong. Stay out of it."

Crap, he had a point. Bonnie's death had not been accidental. It had been violent, and I shuddered at the memory. "How did you know I'd been...investigating?" I demanded, finding it incredibly difficult to accept being told what to do.

"It's my job." His reply was as enigmatic as his face, revealing nothing.

"You're a lawyer, not a cop," I pointed out, but the sly grin sliding across his face told me there was more to him than that. "How do you know Dad anyway?" I decided to tackle the mystery that was Blake Tennant from another angle.

"Your dad and I go way back." He leaned back in his chair, idly turning his cup between his fingers.

"Where did you meet?"

"At a job."

"He was a client?" I pressed.

"Come on, Harper, you know I can't reveal that." Oh right—client confidentiality and all that crap. I leaned forward, resting my elbows on the table. Gran had been uncharacteristically quiet throughout our exchange but now she piped up with, "You married?"

"Gran!"

"What?" she protested. "It's a fair question. No point you being all googly-eyed over him if he's taken." Once more, a blush heated my face and I feared this was my go-to reaction around him—red-faced.

"No ma'am, I am not." Blake's grin was wolfish and when he winked at me, I nearly self-combusted.

"Excellent news." Gran beamed at him. "You'll do nicely for our Harper here. She's been a bit...unlucky... in the love department."

"Oh my god, Gran, shut up!" I had never felt more embarrassed in my life.

"Is that right?" He was enjoying this. I had the urge to hit him, curling my fingers into fists in preparation.

"Her loser fiancé in East Dondure was cheating on her. Took her long enough to see the real him, I have to tell you," she grumbled. "Then she's been mooning over Jackson, knowing full well he has a girlfriend."

I shot to my feet, my humiliation complete. To think, mere minutes ago, I'd been celebrating that Gran was out of jail. Now I wish she were locked away in that cell, far away from Blake Tennant, where she couldn't blab about my entire life history. I didn't know what to do or say. I could see the speculative gleam in Blake's eyes and the cunning glint in Gran's, and I'd had enough.

Without a word, I stalked out of the café and across the road to The Dusty Attic, vowing to never speak to either of them again.

SIX

Fire licked at the sky, orange tendrils dancing and swaying in the evening breeze. It was our coven's blessing ceremony and I'd had to relax my stance on not talking to Gran. Who was I kidding? As soon as she'd pranced into the store an hour later, talking a mile a minute about her adventures in jail, I'd given in. Who could stay mad at her? And I knew she meant well, it's just...did she have to be so damn embarrassing about it?

Standing in a circle, hands clasped, the moonlight shining down on us, I let my gaze linger on my coven sisters. To my left were the oldies—Gran, then Annie, and Agnes. To my right, the younger crowd—Jennifer, and Leah, the youngest of our coven at twenty-six.

Annie led the ceremony, calling to the power of the earth, air, fire, and water, binding us in the circle. Then she led a prayer, asking for a blessing from the Goddess for Gran, not only for the trouble she was currently in, but to bring her success at the Decadent Desserts competition. Thankfully, our ceremonies were mercifully brief. Annie was of the belief that the Goddess was plenty busy enough that we didn't have to call on her for hours on end, boring her with our tales of woe.

"Your Gran wasn't lying when she said you were powerful." Annie approached me after the ceremony was over. The witches had other things on their mind, like drinking wine and dancing around the fire now that the formalities were out of the way.

I inclined my head. "Thank you." I was getting used to my magic, and of the idea that I was stronger than any witch in our coven. None of them could do magic empty-handed, they required a wand to channel and amplify their power.

"Your grandmother tells me an equally powerful fae is in town," Annie continued, watching me carefully.

"A fae? Who?" This was the first I'd heard of it.

"You've met him, I believe."

She had to be talking about Blake Tennant. Yet I hadn't known he was fae. Why was that?

"Ahhh." Annie nodded. "You didn't know? He must have been masking it. I'm sure Drixworths will teach you how to mask your magic too—it can come in handy."

"How did Gran know?"

"She asked him." I blinked at that. So, Gran had outright asked him if he was a paranormal and he'd told her? I couldn't even get him to tell me how he knew my dad.

"She could sense he was a paranormal but not his species. You know Alice, she has a way of getting you to spill all your secrets." Annie grinned and I smiled half-heartedly in return. It was true, Gran had a special charm all her own all right.

"Powerful, you said?"

"Only a certain few can mask their power like that."

"And I'm one of them?" I kicked at the dirt, making a mental note to ask Izzy the next time I saw her.

"You and he together could be—"

"Annie, get over here!" Gran yelled, interrupting us before Annie could finish her sentence. Annie touched my arm. "We'll talk later." Then she was gone, joining Gran and Agnes as they poured wine into Dixie cups.

Sighing, I turned my back, pulling my coat tighter to my neck. The days were getting warmer, but the temperature plummeted when the sun went down, and my breath was puffing in white clouds in front of my face.

"Here." Leah Griffith, the youngest member of our

coven, shoved a hip flask into my hand. "You look like you need it."

"Thanks." Lifting the flask to my lips, I took a gulp, the rum burning my throat and warming me. I held it out to Jennifer.

"Your Gran seems to be holding up okay," Jennifer said, as the three of us sat huddled on a log, our backs to the merriment going on behind us.

"She is amazing," I agreed. "I know she and Bonnie had their differences, but she didn't kill her. Which reminds me"—I leaned in close—"do either of you know if Bonnie was seeing anyone? Romantically, I mean."

"I heard rumors that she was dating Vernon Garza, but they'd broken up," Leah said, and I snapped my head to look at her in the darkness.

"Really?"

She shrugged. "Oh yeah, this was before you moved home. Turns out, Vernon was dating both Bonnie and Bernice...and Bonnie found out about it and wasn't happy."

"Bernice? As in, Bernice Kemp?" Bernice was another member of the Crescent Coven. I imagine it wouldn't have gone well that two members of the coven were dating the same man.

Leah nodded. "Yep. I think Vernon and Bernice may still be dating, I'm not sure."

Jennifer piped up, "I saw them having coffee together at Bean Me Up last week."

Meow! Archie stood on his hind legs and stretched up my leg, clawing at me.

"Ready to go, buddy?" I asked, reaching down to scratch his ears. I refused to turn around to address the witches dancing around the fire, knowing full well by now, they would be naked. I'd only made that mistake once, and the memory was burned in my brain.

"Gran?" I called. "You staying here tonight?"

"Sure am, doll." Silence, then a giggle. *I will not look, I will not look.* "I'm taking Archie home. I'll see you tomorrow."

"We'll see you at the ball tomorrow night, Harper," Annie and Agnes chorused together.

"You will," I agreed in way of farewell. "You two coming?" I asked Leah and Jennifer who were passing their flask back and forth. Seems I was the only witch not intent on getting plastered out of her brain tonight, but both women jumped up and followed me out of the woods behind Annie's house.

After giving Leah and Jennifer a lift home, I headed back to Gran's. It was early, only just nine o'clock, but I was exhausted. Still, there was packing to be done. Tomorrow, I collect the keys for my rental of the caretaker's cottage up at the lighthouse. Although, as I stood in the kitchen, with packing tape and scissors in hand, I wondered if I should delay moving out? Gran needed me, and moving out now seemed a bit heartless.

Still, it wouldn't hurt to get some packing done—not that I had much. Most of what I'd left behind in East Dondure in the apartment I'd once shared with Simon had arrived in boxes that had barely survived the trip. I hadn't contacted him to ask for my stuff, but it had arrived out of the blue early in the new year. When I opened a couple of the boxes, I'd cringed at the way my beloved belongings had been packed. Not so much as packed but shoved into a box with little regard for their welfare. There had been no note. Nothing.

I'd been tempted to call. A moment of weakness, of wanting to hear his voice, of knowing at that point in time—even if he *was* throwing my things into boxes willy nilly—he'd been thinking of me. I'd weathered that storm by giving my phone to Gran, with strict instructions not to return it to me until the following day. Then, Jenna and Monica had come over and we'd watched Hallmark movies and got shit-faced drunk. My lips twitched at the memory. It had been a good night—a great night even—despite the killer hangover the next day. I'd gotten through without contacting my cheating ex-fiancé.

Doubting the boxes my stuff had arrived in would survive another trip, I knew I needed to either repack or repair them. Either way, I'd be moving out at some point, even if it wasn't tomorrow. May as well be prepared. Plus, it gave me something to do. As tired as I was, I also felt wired. Pretty sure if I headed up to bed now, I'd lay staring at the ceiling for hours on end.

I was in the kitchen searching for a sharpie to mark the boxes when I heard a noise outside the kitchen window. Pulling back the curtain, I peered out but couldn't see anything in the darkness. Out the corner of my eye, I saw Archie streak past and then the sound of the cat door flapping as he shot through it.

"It had better not be that sneaky shapeshifter again!" Drixworths had sent one to spy on me when I'd first returned to Whitefall Cove, only the shifter had been a mouse and Archie kept catching him. He should be grateful he'd escaped any serious injury—he could have ended up inside Archie's belly.

What if it isn't the mouse shifter though? Refusing to cower inside, afraid of every little noise, I snatched up a saucepan as a weapon and made my way to the back door, flipping the catch and easing the door open.

I couldn't see squat so I reached back in to turn on the porch light. Standing on the back porch, saucepan clutched in my hands, I scanned the garden. No sign of anyone or anything. Not even Archie.

"Who's there?" I shouted, proud my voice didn't wobble. At my yell, the insects went quiet and I got that prickly sensation you get when someone is watching you. "Come out!"

I took a hesitant step forward until I was at the edge of the porch and at the top of the stairs. With my heart thundering in my chest I made my way down the three steps to ground level. I wasn't sure what I'd do if someone was hiding and did come out. Scream and run away, most likely. But they didn't know that.

My bravery was fading fast, and the saucepan trembled in my hands as I snuck around the side of the house. The porchlight didn't reach this far, and darkness enveloped me. What was I thinking? Quickly regretting my brash actions and deciding it was far safer inside the house—with the lights on—I almost jumped out of my skin when something brushed against my leg.

Meow?

"Jesus, Archie." I breathed out a shuddering breath. "You scared me, boy!" I bent to rub my hand along his back, smiling when he arched beneath my touch. "Let's go inside, shall we?" As I turned, I walked straight into a brick wall. A warm, breathing, wall.

"Yaaaaaa!" I swung the saucepan high and wide, connecting with a solid *thunk.*

"Ow!" the human wall complained, grabbing hold of my wrist to prevent me from swinging again. "Jesus, Harper. Quit it, would you?"

"Blake?" Peering closely in the dim light, I could just make out his face looming over me. "What are you doing skulking around in the dark?" I demanded, my heart rate nowhere near to a normal rhythm. He'd scared the living daylights out of me. With my free hand, I shoved against his chest, putting space between us.

"Checking up on you." His voice didn't reveal anything. Not concern. Not remorse. I blew out a breath, unexpectedly irritated he'd felt the need to not only check up on me but scare me half to death.

"You'd better come in. Let me look at that head." I pushed past him, angry. He deserved a smack in the head with a saucepan. As I stormed inside, I felt him close behind me, heard the door close, and the lock click. "I can take care of myself, you know. I'm not some useless female who needs protecting."

My anger rose with each word and I could feel myself becoming more and more wound up. I ignored him each time he said *Harper* in that resigned way, and knew he was shaking his head even without looking at him. Which annoyed me even more. What was he really doing here? I didn't need protecting—and what did he think he was protecting me from? There had been no threats, no one was out to get me.

"Harper!" His sharp tone finally caught my attention and I swung around, saucepan still in hand. "What?!"

Then I saw the blood oozing between his fingers where he held his hand to his head. All the blood left my face and I felt my stomach turn over. *Oh god.*

"Don't freak out."

Too late. Tears welled in my eyes until he was a blurry blob. A bleeding blurry blob. I'd done this. I'd hurt him, made him bleed. I was an awful person. Tears rolled down my face as the saucepan slid from my hand and hit the floor with a *thwack*.

"Jesus," Blake swore.

Oh god, this was so humiliating. I wasn't normally a crier, but here I was, with the waterworks not showing any signs of abating. Wiping my running nose on my sleeve, I turned my back and drew in a shuddering breath, trying to get myself under control.

"Come here." Blake pulled me against his chest and ran a hand up and down my back in a soothing gesture. "Heaven only knows why you're crying. You're the one who hit *me*," he grumbled, but I heard the teasing note in his voice.

I giggled, the sound muffled. We stood like that for long minutes, his hand running up and down the length of my back while I hiccupped against his chest before I finally dragged in a deep breath and stepped back.

"Quit blubbering and let me take a look at that head," I said, hurrying over to the cupboard that housed the first aid kit, keeping my back to him while I wiped my fingers under my eyes.

He chuckled. "I'll let you have that one, Jones."

"Thanks. Big of you." I turned with the first aid kit

in hand, stopping and taking in his big frame that was currently dwarfing one of Gran's kitchen chairs. His hands were resting loosely on the table top, one of them stained with blood. I felt the color leave my face as my eyes sought out the wound I'd inflicted.

"Relax," he cautioned, seeing the look on my face, "it's not bad. Head wounds bleed a lot, that's all."

"But I—"

"Let's not argue about it, huh?" he cut in. "I snuck up on you outside in the dark. You did the right thing. In fact"—he paused, considering—"I'd have been disappointed if you hadn't."

I paused at that. Was he being sincere or merely trying to make me feel better?

"Why were you here anyway?" I asked, pressing a piece of gauze to his head.

"I told you. Checking up on you."

"Why don't I believe you? Why not knock on the front door?" I countered, dabbing at the cut just above his temple. He was right, it wasn't bad, more of a scratch.

"I did knock. You mustn't have heard me. I saw the light on, figured I'd come around the back and check on things."

I rubbed at my temple, feeling a headache coming on. It was true, I hadn't heard him knock—but Archie hadn't reacted to a knock at the door. Why would he lie about such a small thing?

Archie sauntered into the kitchen and headed straight for Blake, sniffing the toe of his shoe before deciding he approved and rubbing against his leg. Blake absently lowered his hand and stroked him.

"You aren't a healer then?" Blake asked, watching as I cleared away the bloody pieces of gauze. The small cut had stopped bleeding and didn't even need a band-aid, although there was a bit of a lump forming.

"No." Some witches had the gift of healing. I was not one of them. Then I remembered what Annie had told me, via Gran—that he was fae.

"Fae can't heal themselves?" I asked, leaning against the kitchen counter with my arms folded over my chest and watched him through narrowed eyes.

He didn't squirm, merely looked at me with those impossibly dark eyes, then said, "I don't have the gift either."

"What *is* your gift?" I pressed. I had a vague understanding of the fae, that they were blessed with different gifts, different powers that as a species, used together, made them very powerful.

"I'm not sure we know each other well enough for this conversation." He'd dodged a direct answer, which only made me want to know all the more.

"What?" I protested. "Your gift is that special you can't tell me? I'm sure Gran already told you my gift is great power. Although, I really don't know what I'm doing with it," I added. So far, all I really knew was I could use my magic without a wand. Convenient? Yes, but hardly earth-shatteringly awesome. Yet, everyone was telling me how powerful I was, and I still didn't know what that really meant.

His eyes crinkled at the corners a second before he smiled, dazzling with his white teeth. His shoulders shook with silent laughter and I almost stomped my foot in frustration. "Why are you laughing?"

He cleared his throat, muttering, "Open book," before sobering and saying, "I was teasing. So, the fae people are blessed with different gifts, as you call them, designed so that we work more effectively together. Mine is energy manipulation. I can control and manipulate energy to use as a weapon—or a shield."

"How come I managed to hurt you then?"

This time, he laughed out loud and pointed to the scratch on his head. "This? This tiny scratch? Oh, honey, you are nowhere near capable of hurting me. Plus, if I'd used a shield, it would have landed you on your ass and I didn't come here to hurt you."

"Why did you come?"

"I promised your dad I'd look out for you."

"I can look after myself." I huffed and he smiled indulgently at me.

"Sure you can. But I promised your dad and when I make a promise, I keep it. But"—he held up a hand when I opened my mouth to argue—"I can see you're fine. Tired, but fine." He stood up, headed toward the kitchen door, and paused with his hand on the frame. "Lock up behind me."

Then he was gone. He'd left via the front door, moving at remarkable speed. By the time I'd stepped into the hallway, the front door was closing. I hurried to slide the bolt across as instructed.

Deciding I'd had more than enough excitement for one night, I climbed the stairs to my bedroom. Packing could wait. Right now, I needed sleep. I'd collect the keys but moving out was on hold.

Archie was already curled into a ball at the foot of my bed and I figured he had the right idea. Sleep now, follow up with leads on Bonnie's murder tomorrow. And, above all else, push thoughts of Blake Tennant out of my head.

"I now call the murder club to order!" Gran clapped her hands, mimicking a gavel, and I shook my head. "Not a murder club, Gran."

"About time you called us." Jenna waggled a finger at me, ignoring the banter between me and Gran. I'd had three missed calls on my phone from her and simply hadn't had a chance to call her back. Until now.

Since it was a Saturday, and the Whitefall Cove Annual Ball was tonight, I'd decided not to open the shop. Instead, I'd called Jenna and Monica, my two best friends, and asked them to meet me at the store. I'd moved the bookcase that had hidden the old case board I'd put together from Whitney's murder and had pinned Bonnie's name in the center. We had a new case, and the stakes were higher than before. Not only was Gran a suspect but they'd arrested her for the murder! I would not rest until her name was cleared.

Monica pulled the blinds, blocking out the sun, before disposing of her big floppy hat, sunglasses, and ankle-length coat. "There, that's better," she said, easing down into one of the armchairs in the reading corner and draping her legs over the side.

"Thanks for coming out during the day," I said, knowing Monica's vampire biology kept her out of the sun most days. Not that the sun would kill her, but it would give her a nasty sunburn in a matter of seconds.

"For you babe, anything," she purred in her sexy-as-sin voice.

Jenna cleared her throat. "Here's what I've got," she said, approaching the board and pinning some notes to it. Jenna was a reporter for the *Whitefall Cove Tribune*, and I was extremely grateful to have her expertise on my side. Jenna had contacts that could prove useful.

On the board, she'd pinned four names. Bernice Kemp, Vernon Garza, Kristen Lane, and Gladys Marquez. Bernice was the other witch Vernon was dating, Gladys was Bonnie's neighbor who'd delivered the eggs, and Kristen Lane was the witch who had found Bonnie's body.

"Hey!" Gran protested. "Why aren't I up there?" She stood with hands on hips, dressed in black stirrup pants—seriously, why are those things still around?—

a yellow boob tube with a hot pink mesh singlet over the top, and a garish floral jacket with shoulder pads that a linebacker would envy. On her feet, instead of her beloved Uggs, she had novelty slippers. Tigers, to be precise.

"Because you didn't kill her," I pointed out. "Therefore, you are not a suspect. Not in my book."

"Mine either," Jenna and Monica said in unison. Gran considered our responses then, apparently satisfied, nodded her head and took a seat.

I leaned on the edge of my desk and studied the names on the board.

"Let me take you through it," Jenna offered, standing by the board and pointing to Bonnie's name. "Bonnie Emerson, seventy-four, head witch of the Crescent Coven. Died by choking. Unconfirmed reports it was the cake she'd intended to enter into the Decadent Desserts competition." We remained silent, each lost in our own thoughts about how Bonnie had died. Jenna continued.

"Kristen Lane, twenty-seven, fellow member of the Crescent Coven, discovered Bonnie's body at approximately five p.m. Thursday afternoon. She'd called in to pick Bonnie up and give her a lift—the Crescent Coven had their blessing ceremony that night."

"Kristen's grandmother, Delores Lane, is next in line to be head witch of the Crescent Coven," Gran said. "Maybe she did it. Got tired of waiting to be top dog, decided bumping Bonnie off was faster than waiting for her to kick the bucket in her own sweet time."

"Interesting," Jenna commented, but jotted down Delores' name with a question mark and pinned it beneath Kristen's. "We'll have to explore that angle some more."

She continued with her presentation. "Then we have Bernice Kemp. Yet another member of the coven and also dating Vernon Garza—our other suspect."

"I hear that Vernon had also been dating Bonnie on the sly," I said, "and that Bonnie and Bernice didn't know he was dating the other."

"Oh really?" Jenna narrowed her eyes in thought. "Here's a big motive. A love triangle!" She moved the pins around so Vernon was at the top and Bonnie and Bernice beneath, forming a triangle.

"So maybe Bernice got wind that he was dating Bonnie and decided to remove the competition—"

"Or Vernon did away with Bonnie. Maybe he tried to break up with her and things got out of control?" Monica piped up, tapping her ruby red lips with a slender finger.

I cleared my throat. "We've got plenty of motive on this board, but little evidence. I can tell you that we found the remnants of burned love letters in Bonnie's attic."

"From Vernon?" Jenna asked.

I shrugged. "Could be. Jackson took them as evidence. Also"—this time, I aimed my words directly at Gran—"Bonnie's Grimoire is missing."

"Hey," Gran protested, hand to her chest, "don't look at me. I didn't take it. I've got my own. I wouldn't want anything from that coven anyway, the Sisters of the Sacred Flame coven is clearly superior."

"You said *we* found the remnants of burned love letters." Jenna pounced on my slip-up. "Are you saying you were there?"

I bit my lip and nodded. "They'd arrested Gran and I couldn't sit at home twiddling my thumbs. I had to do something, so I went to Bonnie's house to look for evidence. Jackson busted me but let me stay and help. I thought I could sense Bonnie upstairs in the attic— wondered if she was a ghost like Whitney—but instead, there was some sort of orb there. Jackson could see it better than me, he said it can happen when a person crosses over and their magic still... hangs around."

"You know what else can create orbs?" Gran piped up, studying her nails with feigned interest. "Fae."

I caught my breath. Blake had said he manipulated energy. Could he have been behind the orb? Using it to spy on Bonnie? Or us?

"You said yourself he got here awful fast," Gran continued. "After I was arrested, you what? Rang your parents? Who then called him? And a couple of hours later, he was here? Like, he dropped everything for itty bitty me?"

"Oh my god, you're right!" I gulped. My first instinct had been right. The first time I'd laid eyes on Blake Tennant, I'd thought *bad boy*. With a squeaky voice, I said, "Add Blake Tennant to the board. Lawyer."

"Supposedly"—Gran sniffed and I frowned at her—"he got you out, didn't he? There has to be some truth behind who he is."

"Okay, ladies," Jenna soothed, writing out a card for Blake and adding it to the board. "Tell me what you know."

"Ummm." I didn't have much. "He's a lawyer who knows my dad. I don't know how—he wouldn't say."

"Do you have a business card or anything?" Jenna asked. "I can see what I can find out about him and the firm he works for."

I snapped my fingers. "Yes! I do. Hang on." Digging into my purse, I pulled out the card he'd given me and handed it to Jenna.

She looked at it with raised brows. "Did you even read this?"

I shook my head. I'd glanced at it and put it in my purse; my thoughts at the time had been consumed with getting Gran out of jail.

"This business card is from the law firm Richards, Jones, & Tennant."

"He's a partner? A partner is here in Whitefall Cove, defending Gran?" My mouth dropped open. That didn't compute.

Jenna chuckled. "You missed something, Harper."

"There's a Jones in the mix," Monica supplied. "Got any lawyers in the family?"

Richards, Jones, & Tennant. It couldn't be Dad. He's an archeologist. The fact he knew Blake was irrefutable, since Dad had obviously called him and Blake had taken the case with no hesitation.

"Don't panic." Jenna touched my arm, seeing the worry on my face. "I'll look into it. Not hard to get the info on who's who in firms like this. I doubt it's got anything to do with Bonnie's murder, but you want to know who you're dealing with, so leave it with me."

"Thank you, Jenna." I gave her a weak smile, my mind a whirl.

"So, who do you think did it? Who knocked off Bonnie?" Gran demanded.

Jenna, Monica, and I exchanged a look. "No idea," I finally said. "But, we've got one more name to discuss. Gladys Marquez, also a member of their coven and Bonnie's neighbor. Gladys has prolific egg-laying hens and from what I understand, she provides Bonnie with the eggs for her baking, along with selling them at the town markets and privately. There was a fresh bowl on the kitchen table."

"Indicating Gladys had been in the kitchen that day," Monica said.

"Bonnie could have gone next door and collected them," Jenna pointed out.

"Either way, the eggs were fresh. I remember seeing chicken poop and fluffy white feathers stuck to the shells. The two women saw each other that day."

"I think Vernon did it." Gran sniffed. "I think Bonnie caught him with Bernice and kicked his sorry butt to the curb, and he got mad."

"It's a possible theory," I admitted. "But did he have the strength to subdue Bonnie and tie her to a chair in the first place? He's an old man."

"She was an old woman," Gran shot back.

"Yeah, but she's a witch. She had magic to protect herself with," Monica pointed out. "So whoever it was either had magic too, or was physically stronger than her and surprised and subdued her before she had a chance to use her magic."

"Did you find her wand?" Jenna asked and I shrugged.

"I didn't see it in the attic, and I assume if it was in the kitchen or on her body, the police would have it. I guess I can ask Jackson."

"Her wand would be with her. At all times," Gran said.

"Then it has to be at the police station," I replied. "Does it matter?"

"The wand might help you locate the grimoire," Gran said, then swung her oversized, rainbow-colored crochet purse over her shoulder. "Let's go!"

"Go where?" I sighed, just a little fazed by her energy and apparent lack of concern that she was on the hook for murder.

"To go and pay our respects to the Crescent Coven, of course." I must have had a puzzled look on my face because Gran sighed dramatically and spoke slowly and loudly, as if I were impaired.

"We go see Delores Lane, who is now head witch of the Crescent Coven. Say how sorry we are about Bonnie. Ask questions about Bonnie and Bernice dating Vernon."

I couldn't believe it. Gran actually had a good idea and both Jenna and Monica looked a little taken aback as well.

"Right. Yes. We should take some flowers," I said, pushing myself off the desk and grabbing for my bag.

"I'm going to do some digging into Blake Tennant," Jenna said.

"I'm going to get some sleep. I'll see y'all at the ball tonight," Monica said, pulling on her sun shielding apparel. The annual ball was one of the few nights of the year where everything else closed down, which meant Monica, who was a bartender at Brewed Awakening, got the night off.

We selected a bouquet of colorful wildflowers wrapped with a pretty yellow bow, and Gran held them on her lap while I drove us to Delores Lane's house. Delores' house wasn't too far from Bonnie's, just a few blocks to the north, and as I pulled up out the front, I admired the dove gray federation house with white trim. Red brick pavers led up to the porch steps, lush lawn on either side and ample trees and shrubbery.

The first step creaked underfoot as I stepped up, alerting the entire neighborhood it seemed of our presence, for there was a flurry of activity. Front doors opened, curtains twitched, and a shiver ran up my spine. Why did I feel like we were in enemy territory?

The solid black door swung open just as I raised my fist to knock.

"Harper. Alice. What an unexpected surprise," Delores Lane greeted us. Delores was as tall as she was round. Each time I saw her, I thought of the childhood nursery rhyme Humpty Dumpty.

"We've come to pay our respects and say how sorry we were to hear of Bonnie's passing." I waited for

Gran to hand over the flowers and when she didn't, I nudged her, hard. "Gran! Flowers!"

Gran held out the flowers and Delores stared at them, but didn't make a move to take them from Gran, making the entire encounter incredibly awkward. Maybe I shouldn't have brought Gran with me. Maybe this was a bad idea.

"I'm sorry to bother you," I apologized, grabbing Gran's wrist, and was turning away, intent on a hasty retreat, when Delores spoke.

"Won't you come in?"

I froze. That was unexpected. Turning back to her, I gave her what I hoped was a reassuring smile and nodded my head. "Thank you."

The interior of Delores' house was as delightful as the exterior. Dark wooden floors accentuated by white walls and trim. Simple furniture with clear-cut lines and minimal clutter.

"Let's get this out of the way right up front," Gran said, following Delores into the sitting room. "I did not kill Bonnie."

"Of course you'd say that." Delores crossed her arms and frowned at Gran.

"Why would I kill that old bag of bones?" Gran demanded, voice rising. "Nothing in it for me, except a jail cell. And honestly, her angel food cake is not that good—never understood what all the fuss was about."

"How dare you!" Delores straightened her shoulders, her cheeks flushing red.

"Gran! Go and wait in the car!" I pointed toward the front door and Gran looked from the door to me and back again.

"You can't be serious?" she asked incredulously.

"I'm dead serious. Go. I'll be out in a minute."

She eyeballed me for a minute, but I didn't back down, not even when that steel-like stare cut through me and made me doubt the wisdom of my actions. A small grin curled her lips. "Fine."

She swung on her heel and stomped out, slamming the front door behind her.

"I do apologize," I said to Delores who was now grinning at me.

"No need. Alice and our coven go way back. Sit, child." She waved at the cream-colored sofa and I obediently sank into its plush depths.

"I know Gran can be brash and come off as rude —" I began, but Delores cut me off.

"When I said Alice and our coven go way back, I meant it. I've known Alice forever. And I know she didn't kill Bonnie, that's not Alice's style at all. Where's the fun in beating her in the Decadent Desserts competition if she's dead?"

I visibly relaxed my tense shoulders, relieved beyond measure that Delores believed Gran was innocent.

"So, I assume you're really here to try and find out who did kill Bonnie?" She pulled her wand from the pocket of her smock and waved it. Two glasses of iced tea appeared on the coffee table.

"Well, I'm here to pay my respects, but yes, that too," I admitted, leaning forward to pick up a glass. Delores followed suit, taking a sip of the sweet, refreshing drink.

"What can I do? How can I help?" Clasping the glass to her bosom with pudgy fingers, she looked at me over the rim.

"We've reason to believe that Bonnie was dating Vernon Garza," I said. Delores blinked. "And Bernice Kemp. At the same time," I added.

Delores looked uncomfortable. "Oh dear. We had hoped to keep that quiet," she breathed, picking at the hem of her smock. "That was most unfortunate."

"Can you tell me what happened?"

"Do the police know?" she asked and I nodded. "Then I guess it's only a matter of time before it gets out."

She sighed, taking a sip of tea. "It seems Vernon has been a bit of a cad. He told Bonnie that he and Bernice were no longer seeing each other, so when he asked her out, she said yes. They had a handful of dates, but Bonnie became suspicious when they never went anywhere public. She suspected something was amiss. When she confronted him with it, he confessed that he'd lied—he was still dating Bernice."

"That couldn't have gone down well," I said sympathetically.

Delores grimaced. "Thankfully, not so much a case of a broken heart but wounded pride. Bonnie ended things with him and that's all there was to it."

"Did Bernice know? That he'd been dating Bonnie?"

"Only afterward. When Bonnie threatened Vernon that if he didn't tell her, she would. Bonnie felt Bernice had the right to know the type of man he was, and that if she chose to continue seeing him? Well, then it was a fully-informed decision."

"And did she?" I pressed. "Continue seeing him?"

Delores bowed her head in apparent dejection. "She did. Lord only knows why. Once a cheater always a cheater."

"And this happened recently?"

Tears welled in Delores eyes as she nodded. "A couple of weeks back." She sniffed. "There was such a kerfuffle within the coven, witches taking sides and being mad at Bernice, that Bonnie organized a healing ceremony, to mend any rifts. She had no hard feelings toward Bernice—none of what happened was her fault. Only..." She trailed off.

Only Bonnie had been killed before the ceremony could take place.

"So, when your granddaughter arrived to pick Bonnie up, it was for the healing ceremony? Not a blessing ceremony for the Decadent Desserts competition?"

"That's right. The blessing ceremony was meant to be last night. Of course, now we have no entry, so it's a moot point."

"I'm very sorry." It was truly awful what had happened to Bonnie and I could feel Delores' grief as if it were my own. I finished my drink and rose to my feet, extending a hand to her. "Thank you for talking with me today."

She accepted it, and then winked. "Of course. Please don't consider this a truce between our covens. The fun and games must continue."

With that, she pulled at her wand and tapped my shoulder with it. I was immediately swarmed by a hundred moths.

"Argh!" Swatting at my head and cringing as they flew into my hair, I ran out of her house, arms waving like a mad person.

"What's wrong with you?" Gran asked. She wasn't in the car as instructed, but standing by the bird bath in Delores' front garden.

"Moths!" I yelled, still waving and swatting. Gran laughed. "There are no moths, Harper. She got you, huh?"

I stopped my uncoordinated moth dance and

dropped my arms to my sides. I'd messed up my hair and could feel it in a tangled mess around my head. Oh yeah. Delores had gotten me good. I grinned, then sobered.

"What are you doing?" I asked suspiciously, heading toward Gran. She'd moved to block my view of the bird bath.

"Nothing. Come on, let's get going. You have to collect the keys to the lighthouse cottage, don't you?"

She grabbed my arm and steered me away, back toward the car. I tried to crane my neck over my shoulder, but I couldn't see what she'd done to the bird bath. Considering the spell Delores had just bestowed on me, I decided to let it slide.

EIGHT

The town hall looked amazing, decorated with swathes of fabric hanging from the center of the ceiling out to the sides, and then down the walls. It reminded me of the Arabian nights. Fairy lights were pinned to the fabric and dry ice pumped out over the floor, adding just the right amount of mystery and magic.

Standing in the doorway, I watched as Gran sashayed across the room, her massive hoop skirt swaying. Tonight, she resembled Scarlett O'Hara from *Gone with the Wind*—except for the heavy blue glitter eyeshadow, that is.

Jenna spotted me and hurried over, taking both my hands in hers. She looked me up and down. "You look amazing!"

"Thank you." I beamed. I was in my ruby red

strapless gown, my hair artfully pinned to the top of my head with soft tendrils escaping the pins to rest against my neck. My makeup was on point with winged eyeliner and lips the same shade as my dress. In my hands was my silver clutch with lipstick, keys, and cell phone inside. I had no room for anything else and I wasn't making the same mistake again—I would always carry my phone and keys with me rather than checking them.

"You look pretty good yourself." Jenna was in a midnight blue gown that accentuated her blonde hair and blue eyes to perfection. "Is Monica here yet?"

"She was over with the band a second ago." Jenna pointed and I turned to see Monica in a stunning, skintight dress that clung to her curves from her neck down to her ankles. It was jet black but had a slight shimmer to it, and with her dark hair left loose to cascade down her back, she was a walking dream.

On the stage with the band was a trestle table with the Decadent Desserts entries displayed, and a microphone center stage. Whitefall Cove's big night had arrived and judging by the number of people here, the whole town had turned out.

"Are you okay?" Jenna asked, linking her arm through mine and guiding us across the smoky floor toward the bar.

"I'm fine." I smiled, but I felt it pull on my face like a drying face mask. Tight and uncomfortable.

Jenna stopped. "What is it? Has something else happened?"

"No, nothing like that," I assured her. "It's just, I haven't been able to get hold of Mom or Dad. Gran told me I'm being a worrywart over nothing, they're probably in the air or catching some sleep on a layover somewhere. I just kinda hoped they'd be here by now, you know?"

Jenna rubbed a hand up and down my back in a comforting gesture. "You must miss them. It's been a while, hasn't it?"

"Too long," I agreed. Although we'd kept in touch with video calls, it had been over two years since we'd seen each other in person. Video just wasn't the same.

"Ladies." We were interrupted by Jackson, who appeared in front of us looking jaw-droppingly gorgeous in a black tux, his wavy brown hair brushing his collar and his green eyes sparkling. My mouth watered in appreciation.

"Hi, Jackson," Jenna responded for both of us, "Liliana not with you?"

He shrugged, sliding his hands in his pockets. "She's around here somewhere. Can I get you two a drink?"

"Champagne would be great." I found my voice. And wouldn't you know, as soon as I'd said it, two glasses of champagne appeared before Jackson could even move.

"Your wish is my command," Blake drawled, handing a glass to me and the other to Jenna. "Ladies" —he inclined his head—"you look stunning this evening."

His dark eyes devoured me from head to toe. Forget mouthwatering, my ovaries literally exploded at the sight of him. Despite wearing a tux identical to Jackson, who wore it well, Blake wore it ten times better.

"Thank you." Jenna beamed. "I don't think we've been introduced. I'm Jenna Owens."

"Blake Tennant," he replied, shaking her hand before I could gather my wits and introduce them properly. I'd been too busy having an internal argument with my wayward reproductive organs to remember my manners.

"Didn't expect to see you here tonight," Jackson said to Blake, his voice distinctly chilly.

"I've still got business in town...and I wouldn't miss this for the world," Blake drawled, his dark eyes flicking to Jackson and dismissing him.

"Any idea when Gran's case will be?" I asked. She was on bail, not off the hook, and I felt the weight of it hanging over me.

"As soon as I know, you'll know," he replied, taking a sip of his own champagne and watching me over the rim of the glass. Feeling myself flush under his gaze, I took a hefty gulp. The bubbles went up my nose and the champagne went down the wrong pipe, burning all the way. Coughing and choking, with my eyes streaming, I tried to catch my breath while not spilling my drink, very conscious of the fact I'd just made an absolute twat out of myself.

Jenna took my glass while Blake rubbed my back. How embarrassing. With a throat full of razor blades, I rasped, "Going to the ladies'," and took off as if the hounds of hell were after me. Busting through the bathroom door, my coughs had subsided and I cleared my throat a couple of times before looking at myself in the mirror above the vanity unit. Thankfully, my mascara and eyeliner had stayed put. I dabbed at the dampness beneath my eyes with a tissue and was just finishing up when Jenna arrived.

"You okay?" she asked with concern.

"I'm fine. Went down the wrong way," I explained, smoothing my palms down my thighs.

"So, while I have you alone..." she began, and I gave her my full attention. "Sounds ominous."

She fluffed her hair in the mirror. "It's not. Just wanted to let you know that I looked into Blake Tennant today. He's legit. Definitely a partner. Why he accepted Gran's case, I cannot say. As for the Jones member of the law firm, he—or she—is a silent partner who doesn't practice law. I've not been able to find out any information on who that might be, your father or not."

"Thanks for trying, Jenna." I hugged her, then held her away from me. "I don't want to worry about any of this tonight. Tonight is about having fun. I can hear the music has started, let's go dance. I refuse to hide out in the bathroom."

We exited the bathroom to find the dance floor filling up. The band's first set was jazz. Looking around, I spotted Blake at the bar, one elbow resting on it as he perused the room. Spotting me, he raised his hand, indicating he held my champagne glass. Jackson was nowhere to be seen, swallowed up by the swarm of bodies.

"I can't dance to this," Jenna complained. "Let's wait for the next set. How about we try again with that drink, huh? This time, *swallow* it, don't snort it up your nose."

"Ha ha." I followed her across the floor to where Blake waited, and could feel him watching me every step of the way. It was unnerving and exhilarating, all at the same time.

"Better?" he asked, handing me my drink.

"Much. Thank you."

He looked me up and down, his eyes doing a slow, thorough appraisal.

"Red looks good on you." The corner of his mouth quirked up.

"It matches my cheeks." Oh great. *Brilliant response, Harper.* Blake raised one dark eyebrow at me.

"I meant, because I was red in the face from choking. Not that I go around with a red face all the time. Except when I'm around you, I mean, I feel like I've got constant heat in my face whenever I run into you." Oh. My. God. *Shut up, Harper!* I took a breath, fixed him with a dazzling smile, and asked, "So what are you doing here?"

"Alice invited me."

"She did?" I squeaked. Great. I was back to chipmunk voice. Jenna looked at me with a slightly horrified expression on her face, most likely wondering what the hell I was doing. Normal, intelligent, and most of all, articulate Harper Jones was reduced to a babbling incoherent mess around one slick city lawyer. Taking pity on me, she distracted Blake with a series of law questions, since she was an avid *Law & Order* fan. I listened in, nodded where appropriate, and sipped my champagne, careful not to bring on another coughing fit.

Eventually, the band took a break and a woman dressed in a stylish plum-colored tuxedo, complete with top hat, took center stage.

"Good evening, everyone!" she said into the microphone, her voice loud and clear. "Welcome to the Whitefall Cove Annual Ball and Fundraiser. My name is Donna DeGloria and I'll be your MC for this evening."

A round of applause followed her announcement,

then she waved us into silence. "Thank you, thank you. First of all, I'd like to ask for a moment of silence, in memory of a treasured community member, and reigning Decadent Desserts champion, Bonnie Emerson."

I dutifully lowered my head and sent up a prayer for Bonnie. I nearly jumped out of my skin when a warm hand wrapped around mine. Snapping my head up, I met the sizzling gaze of tall, dark, and unbelievably handsome. Jason Momoa had nothing on Blake Tennant, and to say I was having inappropriate fantasies was an understatement. I didn't know why he'd taken my hand—as a measure of comfort, perhaps—but I didn't pull away. Even though part of me was screaming "Bad boy, bad boy," I couldn't force myself to break contact. So, we stood there, hand in hand, while I silently recited the alphabet backwards just to keep my thoughts at bay.

"And now, on with the show!" Donna declared, making me jump.

"Easy," Blake murmured in my ear, his hot breath dancing over my skin and making me shiver.

"Let me tell you, the judges of the Decadent Desserts had their work cut out for them this year." Donna smiled, waving her arm at the array of desserts on the trestle table behind her. "But there can only be one winner. And this year, that winner is...drum roll, please." The drummer obligingly beat out a drum roll, ending with a clash of symbols. Donna opened a gold-colored envelope, read the contents, then beamed at the audience. "The winner is, Alice Brewer! Congratulations, Alice. Get up here!"

Gran hooped and hollered with excitement, while a distinct murmur of disappointment could be heard from the Crescent Coven witches. I hoped this wouldn't stir up more trouble between the covens. Skirts held high, Gran climbed the stairs at the side of the stage and made her way to the microphone, her smile wide.

"While Alice makes her way up the stage, let me remind you that the desserts will be available for your consumption. Alice's winning entry is the chocolate crepe cake, and folks, I've had a taste myself and it is divine." Gran arrived at Donna's side and she handed over the microphone, along with the Decadent Desserts trophy.

"Thank you, ladies and germs," Gran punned, and a good-natured groan met her greeting. "Y'all know I've been coveting this prize since it began, and that darn witch, Bonnie, kept beating me, year after year."

Closing my eyes on a silent prayer that Gran wasn't about to do or say anything inappropriate or insulting, I subconsciously squeezed Blake's hand. Hard.

"Relax. She's got this," he murmured, not taking his eyes from the stage.

Gran continued, "But I sure as heck didn't want to win because the reigning champion couldn't be here to defend her crown. So," she held aloft the trophy Donna had handed her, "I'd like to dedicate this year's trophy to Bonnie Emerson. May she rest in peace."

My shoulders sagged in relief as applause and whoops of approval reverberated throughout the ballroom. When the noise had settled down, Gran finished, "But watch out next year—the gloves are off. May the best witch win!" And with that, she triumphantly sashayed off the stage with the band serenading her as she left.

Donna took the mic. "Looks like next year's Decadent Desserts is going to be a humdinger!" She grinned. "Okay, folks, get your dancing shoes ready, the band is warmed up and ready to party. The crew will move the desserts to the back of the hall and we'll have a few more sets from the band, and then it'll be time for the Bachelor Auction. Hope you brought your check books!"

The band started back up with a slow, soft rhythm and I jolted when Blake leaned down and whispered, "Let's dance."

With my hand still tucked in his, I didn't resist when he took my champagne from me and placed it on the bar, then led me onto the dance floor. We weren't the only ones affected by the slow, sultry music. Couples swarmed the dance floor, their movements kicking up the dry ice, causing it to move and sway as if it were alive and dancing.

Blake slung one arm casually around my waist, keeping my right hand in his, and began moving slowly with the music. He was graceful on his feet, and it was nice. A little too nice. A heat began to pool just south of my belly button, and I panicked, blurting out the first thing that came into my head.

"Are you afraid of clowns?"

Blake smiled. "No, I'm not afraid of clowns. Are you?"

"A little," I admitted. "I never used to be, not as a kid. But then they started to make scary movies about them, the type of movie that makes me afraid to go to sleep at night. Now I'm a little wary of them."

I was dying here. Why was I talking about clowns, of all things? I clamped my mouth shut and vowed I would not utter another word. That lasted all of thirty seconds.

"Do you like cats? I have a cat. Actually, he's my familiar. His name is Archie," I blurted.

He chuckled. "I know, I met him. At your house. Remember?"

"Oh. Right."

"Relax," he said, pulling me closer. I had a snowball's chance in hell of relaxing when my body was totally fixated on jumping this guy's bones. Then, as we swirled around the dance floor, I caught a glimpse of Jackson and my heart stuttered, just a little.

I'd liked Jackson ever since moving home. Yet, put a tall, dark, and handsome man in my path and my heart switched affections faster than you could blink. Was this me now? Was this who I was after the betrayal of Simon? A flighty, unable-to-make-up-her-mind woman who lusted over more than one man?

"Whatever you're thinking about," Blake murmured in my ear, "quit it. You've gone all tense."

"I was thinking about the case," I lied. Well, not a total lie, because it *was* on my mind.

"How about you leave that to the professionals?" he replied.

I pulled back, staring at him. "You don't know me, not even a little bit," I grumbled. If he did, he'd know I couldn't leave this alone. Not when it was family.

"Oh, I know more about you than you realize," he replied with a smile that had my toes curling and a shiver dancing up my spine. My eternal soul was saved by Gran tapping Blake on the shoulder and asking to cut in. I bowed out gracefully, hurrying back to the bar, leaving the two of them on the dance floor, their heads bent close together.

The champagne from earlier had gone warm so I requested a fresh glass and was taking a grateful sip when Jackson appeared by my side.

"You look lovely this evening," he said, and I smiled at him.

"So do you."

He laughed. "This conversation is giving me deja vu."

I laughed with him, remembering the Christmas Ball when we'd said the same thing to each other. Only then, we'd been investigating Whitney Sims' murder.

"How's the investigation going?" I asked, taking my champagne and moving away from the bar, allowing others access. Jackson followed me.

"Slowly," he replied, shuffling from one foot to the other, before blurting, "Just be careful around Tennant, okay?"

I frowned. "What do you mean?"

"He's a fast-moving, city slicker type of guy. I'd hate to see you hurt."

My eyes widened. Jackson was warning me off Blake? I mean, I should feel flattered—it meant he cared—but instead, I felt a twinge of annoyance.

"Thanks for your concern, but I'm fine. He's Gran's lawyer, nothing more."

"I've seen the way he looks at you, Harper..."

I blinked. Then blinked again. Before I could gather my wits and respond, Liliana appeared, and I marveled at her transformation from austere police officer to sex goddess. She wore a metallic gold dress that accentuated her long, lean figure, and her hair was no longer pulled back tightly but flowing down over her shoulders in lustrous waves. By day, coldhearted cop, by night, sultry seductress.

"There you are." She smiled at Jackson, linked her arm through his, and leaned into his side. Staking her claim. I pressed my lips together. Jackson had no business butting into my love life. And Liliana could relax, I had no intentions of stealing her man.

"Enjoy your evening," I told them both, slipping away, not turning when Jackson called out my name to my departing back.

I was searching for Gran, wanting to congratulate her on her win, when I spotted Kristen Lane out the corner of my eye, dancing with her boyfriend, Cody.

Kristen had found Bonnie's body, and despite having spoken with her grandmother, Delores, a chat with Kristen wouldn't be out of the ordinary. I waited on the sidelines and when the couple left the dance floor, I swooped.

"Hey Kristen." I smiled my friendliest smile. She stopped and returned the smile.

"Oh hey, Harper."

"I was hoping I could talk to you? About Bonnie?"

She looked around, spotted her boyfriend heading to the men's room, then shrugged. "Yeah, okay, I guess. What about her?"

"You found her?"

"Yes." Oh geez. This was like pulling teeth. I placed

my hand on her arm in what I hoped was a soothing gesture. "Would you be able to walk me through it? I want to find who did this to her as much as you do."

Her breath left her lungs in a whoosh and her eyes filled with tears. "It was awful." She sniffled, running her fingers beneath her eyes, wiping away the moisture. "I could sense it as soon as I pushed open the door. Her death. The energy was dark. Evil."

"You pushed open the door? It wasn't locked?"

"When I knocked, it popped open. Like it wasn't properly on the latch. So, I went in and as soon as I set foot over the threshold, I knew something bad had happened." She sniffled again. "I found her in the kitchen. Tied to the chair, her mouth wide open with cake..." She stopped, drew in a shuddering breath, and I ran my hand up and down her arm.

"I'm sorry," I whispered. "That must have been awful."

"Her eyes were open. Glazed," Kristen continued, as if I hadn't spoken, "and just the pure mess of the cake, everywhere. It was everywhere."

"Did you notice anything else? You said the front door wasn't on the latch. What about the back door? Windows?"

She shook her head. "Everything else was shut. There was a note from Gladys on the egg bowl. Flour and butter and milk on the table from where she'd been baking."

"So, the cake, the one that was used to...you know...you think that was her entry in the Decadent Desserts competition? Or a practice run?"

Kristen straightened her shoulders and dragged in another deep breath. "It was her entry. It had to be. There wouldn't have been enough time for another—she slow bakes, says that's one of the secrets—oops." She clapped a hand over her mouth, her eyes wide in horror.

"It's okay," I soothed. "I'm not interested in her baking secrets. My lips are sealed, I promise."

"Thanks," she whispered. "Anyway, that's about it. I ran back out onto the front porch and called the cops. I couldn't wait inside, not with that horrible feeling—it made me feel sick. I didn't want to vomit, not on Bonnie's beautiful garden, but it came close."

I patted Kristen's arm again. "Thanks for talking with me."

"Hey! Get away from her!" Cody appeared, taking Kristen's arm and dragging her away from me.

"It's okay, Cody," Kristen protested, but he was having none of it, bustling her away with a thunderous expression on his face.

"Stay away. Murderer!" he spat.

Oh hey, unfair. This time, it's Gran who's the suspect, not me. But I decided not to argue the point. Kristen flashed an apologetic shrug my way before letting him lead her away.

I spotted Gran over by the trestle table that had been moved from the stage to the back wall of the ballroom and made my way over.

"Congratulations." I kissed her cheek and she winked, her extra-long fake eyelashes brushing her cheek.

"Watch this." She giggled, her eyes on Delores Lane, who was helping herself to the punch bowl on the far end of the dessert laden table.

"What did you do?" Narrowing my eyes, I watched as Delores sipped her drink. She licked her lips then looked down into her cup suspiciously.

Gran whispered, "Prune juice."

Trust Gran to spell the fruit punch. "Change it back. Now!"

"I didn't start it," Gran complained. "Look at them

all twitching out there." She pointed to the dance floor where people were indeed twitching and scratching. "Hope you didn't take one of them sweets from the bar."

I hadn't, but I had noticed the bowl full of sweets sitting on the bar and thought it odd they were there.

Donna DeGloria took to the stage, mic in hand, shushing the band mid-song.

"Sorry for the interruption, folks, but I see our witches are at it again. If you find yourself under the influence of anything other than alcohol, please make your way to the booth out the back where antidotes are being dispensed. Witches, may I remind you that this is a magic-free event." She turned off the mic and the band resumed playing.

"See?" Gran grinned. "Happens every year."

"Well, just quit it, okay?" I mumbled, shaking my head at the witches and their mischief-making ways.

"You're such a goody-two-shoes, a rule follower." Gran patted my cheek, taking any sting out of her words, but she wasn't wrong. Rules were there for a reason, but I couldn't help the grin that escaped when a young man executed a hell of a dance move, trying to scratch his back and leg at the same time.

Gran handed me a paper plate laden with tasty morsels from the dessert table. I squinted at the selection. "They aren't spelled, are they?" I asked suspiciously, not putting it past her.

"Nope, cross my heart." She mimicked crossing her chest. "Oh look, there's Vernon and Bernice." Before I could stop her, Gran had bolted, moving as fast as her hooped skirts would allow. I debated following her but decided to hang back and watch. For now.

Bernice Kemp would have to be in her seventies, at least, and was small. Tiny, in fact, and incredibly slim. She looked as if a stiff breeze would blow her away. Bonnie Emerson had been twice Bernice's size. I couldn't see Bernice being able to physically restrain her. Unless, of course, it was all magic, which we couldn't rule out.

I turned my attention to her boyfriend, Vernon Garza. He had a debonair grace about him, a Frank Sinatra vibe with his gray pinstripe suit and hat dipped low over one eye. He took said hat off to greet Gran, bowing low and sweeping his arm, hat in hand, in front of him. He had a full head of gray hair that matched his moustache. Vernon was one hundred percent human, and of average height and build. I tilted my head and pondered the possibility of whether this elderly gentleman had the strength to restrain Bonnie. What if they'd done it together? Bernice's magic combined with Vernon's physical strength.

"They have an alibi," Jackson said beside me, making me jump. "Sorry, didn't mean to startle you."

With my hand on my chest to calm my thundering

heart, I glanced at him before turning my attention back to the elderly couple.

"Oh?"

"They were at the cinema. Ticket stubs prove it."

"Ticket stubs prove they were there, not that they stayed for the entire movie," I pointed out.

"True. Although we have witnesses seeing them leave. It was a double feature, started at three o'clock, got out at seven. They went to dinner afterward."

Damn. Bonnie was killed within that timeframe. "They could have snuck out and back in again," I said.

"Little bit difficult at their age, but yes, I suppose so." He was humoring me.

"And you're sure Bonnie has crossed over?"

"You were with me at her house. No sign of her there. I don't like to do séances anymore—last time I did that, I got inundated with ghosts wanting me to pass on messages. Took me six weeks to get rid of them, one by one."

I found his necromancy talent fascinating. I couldn't fathom what it would be like to see ghosts. "Are there any here?" I asked, looking around the ballroom, wondering if they were here, joining in.

Jackson glanced around the room, his eyes shot back to a place at the foot of the stage, stayed there for a second, before moving on.

"You saw one, didn't you?" I pounced, casting my

own gaze to the spot I'd seen him zoom in on. "There's a ghost here. Who is it?"

He shrugged. "I don't know. It's a woman, she's wearing a long dress, with an apron. Like an old-fashioned maid's outfit, maybe. It's hard to say, she's incorporeal so there's not a whole lot of detail."

"What's she doing?"

"Standing there, wringing her hands."

I frowned. Wringing her hands? Sounded like she was worried. "Do you need to help her?"

"Shh." He shushed me and I frowned. "She's seen me. She knows we're talking about her. Keep quiet, she's coming over."

"Coming over?" I squeaked, wringing my own hands. I kept my eyes trained in the direction I thought she'd be coming from and almost fainted when an apparition began to take shape. The closer she got to us, the more I could see her.

"Oh my god," I breathed. "It's happening again. Being with you makes me see ghosts."

She was gliding across the room, her feet a foot off the floor. My heart was beating double time in my chest. I did not like ghosts. I could tolerate Whitney haunting my bookstore, possibly because I knew her, but it still gave me the heebie jeebies.

My skin prickled with goose bumps as the ghost drew near and I felt chilled to the bone. Without thought, I grabbed Jackson's hand. His flesh was warm and comforting and he wrapped his fingers securely around mine.

"Take a breath, Harper," he muttered, "Don't want to draw attention to ourselves. It's always awkward talking with a ghost in public."

Oh. Right. Of course. No one else could see her. I couldn't continue to stand by Jackson's side, holding his hand, if he didn't want to appear like he was talking to thin air. Reluctantly, I released my death grip and shuffled around so I was facing him. There. Now it would at least look like he was talking to me.

The ghost drifted in between us and to say it was disconcerting to see right through her was an understatement. I waited for her to speak, shifting from one foot to the other. Then, without uttering a word, she disappeared. I sagged, from relief or disappointment, I wasn't sure.

"Did she say something and I just didn't hear it?" I asked, regaining my composure.

Jackson shook his head. "Nope. Sometimes it's like that. She just came over to check me out, see if I was a threat or not. I'm guessing not since she left without any trouble."

"They give you trouble?"

"Sometimes. Some are malevolent."

"What do they do?" I was all ears.

"They can't physically hurt me, but they can use objects to hurt me."

"Like what?"

"Strong ones can pick up objects to throw at me. Like chairs."

"Could they restrain you?"

His green eyes narrowed. "I see where you're going with this, and no. Even a malevolent spirit can't tie me to a chair and shove cake in my mouth."

"Okay, okay, it was just a thought." The truth was, I was having a hard time believing any of the old witches who were suspects in Bonnie's murder were physically capable of such a feat. Which left Kristen Lane as my only viable suspect. What if she'd killed her, then called the cops? They wouldn't suspect her since she claimed to have discovered the body. I was about to question Jackson about it when a voice I thought I'd never hear again called my name.

"Harper! Harper! There you are." It was as if the world stopped. The entire ballroom went silent, and I was in a bubble with no sound as I slowly turned and watched as Simon made his way toward me. Of course, the ballroom wasn't really silent. Everything was continuing on as normal, it's just my ears had stopped listening. Suddenly, it all came back in a deafening rush.

"So glad I finally found you." He grabbed my shoulders and dropped his head to kiss me. I quickly turned away before he could connect, his lips brushing awkwardly across my cheek as I stepped backward, out of reach.

"What are you doing here?" I asked, proud my voice didn't tremble.

"Looking for you." He was dressed in jeans and a blue sweater I hadn't seen before. It was a stark reminder that this man, my ex-fiancé, had moved on without me. Once upon a time, I'd been intimately aware of every single item of clothing in his wardrobe. Not anymore.

"We have nothing to talk about Simon," I said, crossing my arms over my chest. "I suggest you leave."

"Simon?" Jackson cut in, not missing a thing. "As in, cheating ex-fiancé Simon?"

"The one and only," I replied, voice dripping ice.

"Oh, that's so mature, Harper." Simon rolled his eyes. "I would have thought more of you than to slander me to your friends."

Jackson's chest puffed out and he wedged himself between us, forcing Simon to step back.

"I'd watch your tone, buddy," he growled, full-on protective cop mode locked and loaded.

"Who's this?" Simon sneered, peering at me around Jackson's bulk. "Your new boyfriend? You didn't waste any time."

Oh, the nerve of him.

"This is Detective Jackson Ward of the Whitefall Cove Police Department," Jackson replied menacingly.

"I'd advise you to *watch your tone*. And no, I'm not her boyfriend."

Our little encounter was starting to draw attention because suddenly, I was flanked on either side by Jenna and Monica, and Gran was approaching fast. My eyes welled with tears that they had my back, for despite outward appearances, I was shaken that Simon had shown up.

"Is this him?" Jenna asked, eying Simon with distrust, and I nodded.

Simon stepped around Jackson and held his hand out to Jenna. "Simon Lancaster. Harper's fiancé."

I gasped at his audacity. Jenna didn't accept his hand, just stared at him hard. He swallowed before turning his attention to Monica. She took his hand and smiled a smile that was so chilling I shivered. "Simon Lancaster. I've heard terrible things about you," she drawled.

"You have?" This time, it was his turn to squeak and my lips twitched. *Good. Squirm, you bastard.*

Monica nodded, squeezing his hand, watching as he winced and sweat dotted his forehead. "You're the cheating bastard who broke Harper's heart. You don't get to come to this town, to her home, and claim her as yours."

"Y-y-you're right," he stammered, desperately trying to retrieve his hand, but Monica wasn't budging, and with her vampire strength keeping his hand trapped in hers, crushing it was effortless. She could do this all night. For once, Simon clued in pretty quickly. "I apologize," he gasped.

I elbowed her and she released her grip just as Gran arrived.

"This him?" Seemed Simon didn't need an introduction at all. I nodded. Before I could even guess her intent, Gran pulled her wand from her cleavage and sparks flew as she aimed it at Simon.

Just as I gasped, "Gran," and tried to stop her, he suddenly yelped. Oh my God, what had she done? I was already in trouble with Drixworths for using magic to harm a human, the last thing I needed was another infraction.

I looked at Simon and couldn't contain the laugh. He stood there in his tighty-whities and nothing else, hands clasped over his crotch.

"Real mature!" he yelled, face red. "So, what's next? A wedgie?"

"Nah, I think you've got enough stuck up your butt." Gran tucked her wand away, dusting her hands together.

"Whatever, freak show," he snapped.

"Simon"—I finally found my voice—"I don't believe you've met my grandmother."

He shut his mouth with an audible snap.

"Harper, can we please go someplace to talk." He turned beseeching eyes to me and for a nanosecond, I almost capitulated. Then I remembered my own humiliation, the recollection of another woman's legs wrapped around him in the cloak closet. The memory of my own pain and humiliation scorched my cheeks and I felt my magic dance across my knuckles. A big hand wrapped around my clenched fist.

"Easy," Blake said into my ear. He knew. He knew the power that was roiling through me, tumultuous and uncontrollable. I felt it clawing at me for release, to do more to Simon than turn him into another creature, to inflict the pain I'd felt at his hand. Blake's other hand slid around my neck to rest at my nape, softly stroking, massaging, easing the tension.

It worked. He soothed the savage beast within and I slumped back against his chest. Simon's beady eyes didn't miss any of it. He opened his mouth and I braced myself for more vile words, but Blake beat him to it.

"Zip it," he ordered, his voice ringing with authority. "She doesn't want to speak with you. She doesn't want to see you. Take your repulsive pale-skinned body out of here and don't come back."

"You can't speak for her," Simon spat out, the face I'd once thought handsome, twisted and bitter.

"I'm done, Simon. With you," I said, my voice level, calm. I was stronger without him than I was with him. "You should leave. Don't come back. There's nothing for you here."

He blinked at me, shocked beyond measure at my rejection. I turned to Gran. "Please return his clothes. I suspect his keys were in his pocket and I'd really like *not* to give him an excuse to stay."

"Fair enough, doll." Gran whipped out her wand and bestowed Simon with his clothes. He tugged at the neckline of his sweater and swept a glance over all of us before hurrying away.

Jenna threaded her fingers with mine and pulled me away. "Come on. There are shots at the bar."

"**S**he did what?" I asked, mouth agape. Standing on the doorstep before me was Blake Tennant dressed in jeans and a blue T-shirt, and looking more delicious than a man had a right to.

"Alice won me in the bachelor auction"—he grinned—"and gave me to you. Don't you remember?"

No. I did not remember. Because I'd gotten shitfaced drunk after Simon left. Jenna and Monica had kept up protective duty around me for the rest of the night. We'd drank, danced, and drank some more. Today, I had the mother of all hangovers to prove it.

"You look better than I expected." Blake looked me up and down, and I couldn't even summon the energy to be offended. I was pretty sure I looked as awful as I felt. I'd pulled on a pair of sweat pants and T-shirt, sans bra, and half-suspected last night's makeup was now smeared over my face since I hadn't bothered with the whole cleansing routine before flopping into bed.

"Your hair, however, could use some help." He reached forward and began plucking pins from my locks, apologizing when I winced. "Slept with it like this, huh?" He grinned, finally freeing all the strands and running his fingers through them.

"I guess." Proof that I was probably still drunk because ordinarily, I would have been mortified to have him see me like this.

"Your Gran said you were moving and could use the muscle power. Are you going to let me in?"

I sighed, pushed the door open so he could enter. "Sure. Why not," I grumbled, heading down the hallway to the kitchen where I'd been nursing a mug of black coffee and pushing pancakes around my plate with a fork.

"You got something to tell me?" I asked Gran, sliding back into my seat and ignoring the way my stomach was turning at the thought of food.

"Oh good, you're here," she said to Blake. "Pancakes?"

"Sure." He sat opposite me and I glared at the comfortable comradery he had with Gran. Like they were best friends from way back.

"You didn't tell me about this," I said to Gran, pointing my fork at Blake.

"Didn't I? Must have slipped my mind," she shot back and I narrowed my eyes at her.

"Look." I gulped down a mouthful of coffee. "While I appreciate the gesture and all"—I gestured to both of them—"I don't need the help. I have a handful of boxes, that's it."

I'd picked up the keys for my new rental yesterday and told Gran of my reservations about moving out given she was on the hook for murder. She'd solved that problem by pretty much kicking me out of the house, telling me she loved me to the moon and back but apparently, I was cramping her style. Seemed she was more than ready to have her house back to herself, and we agreed I'd move today. It was Sunday, I didn't have to open The Dusty Attic, and it would give me a day to settle in to my new place. I hadn't expected Gran to buy a bachelor from the auction to assist. Then a thought hit me.

"Who else did you bid on?" I demanded, not remembering the details of last night's events. I had a vague recollection of doing my own bidding, only to have Jenna and Monica pin my arms to my sides—for my own protection, they'd told me.

"All of them!" She grinned, winking at me.

"Did you win any others?" I pressed, and Blake barked out a laugh before Gran shushed him.

"Don't tell her. I'd like to leave her stewing for a bit."

It was all the motivation I needed to finish breakfast and get packed and out of here. If there were going to be a stream of men coming through the front door, I'd prefer not to be here when it happened.

"Ready for my help yet?" Blake asked, and I tossed my napkin on the table in resignation.

"Okay, fine. It'll be quicker with two of us, we can probably get it done in one trip." I stood up. "Finish your breakfast," I told him. "I just have some last-minute stuff to finish packing, then I'm set."

Rushing upstairs as fast as my hungover body could manage, I could hear the murmur of their voices and wondered again how Blake knew my dad. I'd pressed Gran on it but she'd said this was the first time she'd met Blake and to ask my father. I would if I could. I glanced at my phone for the millionth time. Why couldn't I get ahold of them? I'd started checking the news every hour for word of plane crashes, but so far, nothing. Maybe it was like Gran had said, they were on a layover somewhere and their phones were dead.

I was packing my toiletries and the last of my clothes into my suitcase when my phone chimed. Finally! Swiping at the screen, expecting to see a text from Mom or Dad, I was somewhat disappointed to see Jackson's name. I opened the message.

"Need a hand moving today?"

My eyes narrowed. How did he know? *Gran.* I

wondered if she'd bid on him too. I'd seen his name in the list of eligible bachelors and had figured Liliana would have outbid anyone who'd dared to try to win a date with her man.

"Got it covered, thanks."

Then I remembered I had something I'd wanted to ask him and fired off another message.

"There was a note?"

My phone rang. It was Jackson.

"Who told you that?" he asked without preamble.

"Kristen Lane. She said there was a note from Gladys on top of the egg bowl. It wasn't there when I —" I paused. I'd been about to say broke in, but hurriedly added, "I didn't see it when I was there. Do the police have it?"

"When you broke in, you mean." Jackson chuckled. "Yes we have it, and yes, it was from Gladys, wishing Bonnie good luck in the competition."

"Oh." I don't know what I'd been expecting, that it had been a confession or something. I guess they wouldn't have arrested Gran if that had been the case. I felt somewhat deflated.

"Harper?" Jackson said, snapping me out of my stupor. "I said, are you sure you don't need a hand today. Your Gran said you were moving."

"I've got it covered, but thank you." I smiled, touched that he'd offered.

"You finished packing yet?" Blake said from the doorway and I glanced at him over my shoulder.

"Almost. You can start with those boxes." I pointed to where four boxes sat stacked against the wall.

"Tennant's there?" Jackson asked, voice sharp.

"Yes. Gran won him in last night's auction and volunteered him to help with the move," I explained.

"I would have helped." He sounded...jealous. But that couldn't be. Why would Jackson be jealous that Blake was helping me? Men were so damn confusing.

"I really don't need any help," I said. "I've literally got six boxes and a couple of suitcases. It will take ten minutes, tops. Blake wouldn't be here if Gran hadn't interfered."

"Right." He sounded weird and I frowned.

"Is everything okay?" I asked.

"I'm fine. I'll see you around." And he hung up.

"Trouble in paradise?" Blake asked, and my frown grew deeper.

"Why would you say that?" I asked, and Blake outright laughed.

"You can't be that naïve," he said, hefting two boxes into his arms and heading out the door. "That man has the hots for you. Only he's too much of a pussy to say so. And he's too whipped by that girlfriend of his to do anything about it."

"What?!" I yelled after him, but all I heard was the

thumping of his feet on the stairs and his laugh echoing behind him.

All my angst over Jackson and Blake melted away when I turned the key in the lighthouse cottage lock and the door swung open. I was home. Stepping over the threshold with Archie in my arms, I felt the cottage embrace me as if it had been waiting all this time— just for me. Much like The Dusty Attic had.

"Nice place." Blake followed me inside, his eyes taking in the hardwood floors, white shiplap walls, and beach décor. Through the large living room window stood the lighthouse, majestic in its splendor. No longer in operation, it remained a tourist drawcard in the summer. And now I lived in the old caretaker's cottage. With a smile on my face, I spun in a circle until Archie meowed and demanded to be put down.

"Sorry, boy!" I lowered him to the floor where he immediately began exploring, sniffing every available surface. The cottage was a simple two-bedroom design. It was cozy, with the living room, kitchen, dining room, and half-bath downstairs, and two bedrooms and the main bathroom upstairs. I couldn't believe my good fortune in not only renting it, but renting it furnished.

Blake had half the boxes in his rental car and half

were in mine, so I'd been right, it only took us one trip. What I really wanted to do was start unpacking and possibly lounge on the sofa, but with Blake here, it felt awkward, like I had to entertain him.

"Seriously, Harper, you've gotta learn how to school your face," he drawled, standing in the doorway with his hands behind his back. I did my best to wipe the guilty look from my face but from the way his lips twitched, I could only imagine I wasn't very successful.

"Thanks for your help today," I said, trying to be a gracious hostess, "but—"

"But you'd really like me to disappear so you can settle in on your own," he finished for me.

"Something like that." I didn't see the point in lying about it. It wasn't like I'd invited him here. His presence was thanks to Gran's interference, nothing more.

"So, you have no interest in sharing this with me then?" he asked, pulling a picnic basket from behind his back. I blinked, lost for words. "I won it in one of the raffles last night," he explained. "Seems a shame to waste it."

He held the basket out and I walked over to peer inside. It was filled with wine, a selection of cheeses, grapes, strawberries, and crackers, plus more treats, all buried beneath a checkered cloth.

"I figured we could have a picnic up by the lighthouse."

Damn it, he knew my weakness. I glanced out the window at the magnificent white structure on the cliff top. I don't think I'd ever get tired of the view.

"That sounds lovely," I capitulated without a fight. A girl had to eat, didn't she? And I was hungry. I hadn't been able to face food earlier, but my hangover was slowly receding and my stomach growled at the thought of sustenance.

Setting up Archie's litter tray and putting down fresh water and dry food for him, I decided to leave him in the cottage while we were gone. There was plenty of time for him to explore outside later. After locking up the cottage, we strolled side by side up the path to the lighthouse. At the base was a concrete path with steps and surrounding that was lush green grass. I made a note to ask the realtor who kept the grass mowed, because it was very well maintained. Between the lighthouse and the cliff was a park bench and we sat on it with the basket between us.

Blake opened the wine and poured us each a glass while I popped a grape in my mouth. I wasn't sure wine was a good idea but I accepted the glass when Blake handed it to me. "Hair of the dog," he said.

"Do you have a family?" I asked.

"Yes ma'am." He nodded, helping himself to a grape. "I have a sister."

"And your parents?"

"Still alive. Living in Redmeadows."

"And is she a lawyer too? Your sister?"

He chuckled, leaning against the bench, one arm resting along the back behind my head, his legs stretched out in front, crossed at the ankles. "My father is a retired judge. My mom was his secretary. Cliché, I know." He grinned. "And my sister works for the SIA."

"Oh wow. The Supernatural Investigation Agency. That's pretty badass." As an only child, I didn't know what it was like to have a brother or sister to share growing up with, to argue with, play with, laugh with. Not that I had a horrible childhood, far from it, but at times—especially when Mom and Dad were away on a dig—it got lonely, and I'd dream of having a big family.

"Mom always told us we could be whatever we wanted. She didn't care if we were a dog walker or a brain surgeon. To Mom, the most important thing was that we were happy."

"She sounds amazing," I said softly, my eyes on the horizon where the ocean met the sky in a hazy mist.

"She'd like you." His voice was equally soft and I couldn't bring myself to look at him. Last night, he'd rallied around me with my friends, like he was a part of my inner circle. The problem with that was how right it felt. That he belonged. *Don't get used to it, Harper. He'll be leaving soon, remember that.*

We lapsed into silence, each lost in our own thoughts. I heard him rummaging around in the picnic basket, then he nudged my arm. I looked down to see him holding out a sliver of cheese on a cracker. I took it, enjoying the tang of the cheese and the crunch of the biscuit.

"So, about those clowns," Blake said and I laughed out loud.

"Please forget I said anything about clowns," I pleaded.

"Well no, I can't do that," he teased. "Such a riveting topic of conversation."

"Stop." I giggled, my cheeks heating.

"And then it was cats," he continued. "It's got me curious what's going to come out of your mouth next."

"I'm sorry. I babble when I'm nervous," I explained.

"And I make you nervous?"

"Very." *Oh god, Harper, you're doing it again. Just shut up.*

The hand that had been resting on the back of the bench moved to stroke my neck and I shot to my feet, startling us both.

"I don't know what Gran told you, or what you think might happen here, but I can't." I chugged the last of my wine and shoved the glass back into the picnic basket. "Thank you for your help today, but really, I think this…"

He stood and caught one of my hands in his, stilling my anxious gesturing. "Harper." God, even the way he said my name had me coming undone. "Your Gran didn't say anything. There's no hidden agenda here. Just two people enjoying each other's company."

"I don't think I can be trusted," I blurted, and he frowned in puzzlement. "My judgment," I elaborated. "I can't trust myself right now. Seeing Simon last night brought up a whole bunch of stuff."

He looked at me with those impossibly dark eyes. "I would imagine so. Has he bothered you again?"

"No, I haven't heard from him." I wrapped my arms around my waist and turned my back to him, focusing my attention on the ocean.

"Do you want to?" I could feel him behind me, the warmth from his body, but he didn't touch me. He just stood there, and his presence was strangely soothing and equally stimulating.

I shook my head. "No. It's stupid…I'd been longing for at least a phone call. A text message even. Something to say he missed me. But him turning up, out of the blue and unannounced? Well, it made me see something that I don't think I consciously wanted to see. Or know."

"What's that?"

"That, despite the pain and hurt he put me

through, I'm not in love with him. And last night, seeing him in person...he's not the man I thought he was. He had me fooled. And admitting that? It stings."

I hadn't meant to admit that, and panic welled up in me. I had conflicting emotions over Jackson, I'd had the hots in the worst way for Blake, and I wondered if I was merely on the rebound. Either way, my own emotions were too overwhelming and confusing to deal with right now. I'd much rather focus on catching a murderer!

"Thanks for the picnic, but I'm going to head off," I said, not giving him a chance to respond. I hurried down the path as quickly as I could without actually running—because that would look like I was wimping out.

Arriving at the cottage, out of breath but alone, I unlocked the door and stepped inside, managing to catch hold of Archie who'd let out a godawful howling noise and bolted for the door as soon as I opened it. Clutching him tightly and managing to avoid his claws, I ran a hand over his fur which was standing on end. I don't think I'd ever seen him this agitated.

"What is it, Archie?" I ran my hand over his back, stroking until I felt him relax against my chest. "What happened, boy? Did something spook you?"

I pushed the door closed with my foot and moved to the oversized plush sofa, sinking down onto it with Archie on my lap. Then I felt it. Magic.

Power. No wonder Archie was freaked out. Moving him to the cushion at my side, I whispered, "Stay here."

The vibration in the air was similar to what I'd felt at Bonnie's house. There was a dark, sinister undertone. Is this what Kristen had meant when she said she sensed evil?

Whatever it was—ghost, spirit, or something else entirely—it wasn't in the living room. I closed my eyes and centered myself, managing to pinpoint where the energy was coming from. Upstairs, in one of the bedrooms. Making my way upstairs, I paused on the landing, and my eyes zeroed in on the glowing light leaking out from under the door to the master bedroom. I tiptoed across the landing and wrapped my fingers around the knob, and slowly turned. I was trying to be quiet but with a house this old, it inevitably creaks and groans, and that is exactly what it did. The door groaned loudly as I slowly pushed it open.

I gasped at what I saw. The orb. This time, big and bright, I could see it perfectly and it was hovering in my room by my dresser. It turned when I entered, almost as if it could see me, and again, I wondered if it could.

"Who are you? What do you want?" I demanded. It started toward me, slowly at first but picking up speed, and I had flashbacks to Bonnie's attic when it seemed the orb had been about to attack us. Throwing up a hand, I pushed out my magic. "Stop!"

To my utter surprise, it worked. The orb stopped, but by the way it kept backing up and then rushing forward only to bounce back, I imagine my forcefield was an unexpected surprise to the orb as well. Trouble was, we were at a stalemate. I wasn't used to using my magic and holding the orb back was draining me fast. I'd meant to ask Izzy at Drixworths about the orb but I hadn't seen her for my weekly check-in yet. If what Jackson had said was true, someone was using it to spy on witches. I hadn't sensed it at Gran's house, but she had that place warded up the wazoo. No such protection existed here—something I needed to remedy, pronto.

The orb started to emit a loud piercing noise and with one hand thrust out, holding it back, I couldn't cover my ears.

"Harper?" Over the screeching, I heard the front door burst open and Blake yelling my name. I was gritting my teeth so hard I couldn't unlock my jaw to reply but figured he'd worked it out when I heard his footsteps on the stairs.

Within seconds, he was by my side, thrusting his hand, palm out, next to mine and with a *pop*, the orb disappeared. I sagged in relief, bending forward to rest my hands on my knees and drag in a breath. I felt clammy and when I wiped the back of my hand across my brow, it came away damp with sweat. My battle with the orb had been intense and exhausting.

"Thanks," I puffed, straightening up. "We were at an impasse."

"You okay? You look pale." He was too close, messing with my senses again, so I moved over to the dresser and tried to figure out what the orb had been looking at. Or looking for.

"I'm fine. I'm not used to using so much magic." I pulled open the top drawer of the dresser and peered inside. Empty. My suitcases were on the bed, untouched, waiting for me to unpack.

"You aren't?" His eyebrows shot up. "Why?"

"Apparently, my magic is very powerful, and since I kinda neglected my witch heritage for the past five years, Drixworths have me on lockdown. They fear if I'm given full throttle, I could go a little nuts."

He regarded me for a moment. "Interesting," was all he said.

"And that's why I have Archie," I added. "My familiar. He's meant to help me keep a lid on things. Although, I could have used his help with channeling my magic today."

Even though Blake hadn't moved, his eyes had done a thorough inventory of my bedroom. "What do you think they were looking for?" he asked.

"They?"

"Whoever summoned the orb," he prompted. "Clearly, they're looking for something."

"I've seen it before," I blurted. "In Bonnie's attic, the night she died. The night you arrived. I thought it was you."

Not my most eloquent sentence but considering he'd been in the room with me and the orb, clearly, he wasn't the one using it.

"Did you now?" he drawled, dark eyes intent. I swallowed. Maybe I should have kept that observation to myself. "I assume that is no longer your opinion?"

"No," I quickly answered. "I mean, it can't be you. You were here with the orb. You helped me get rid it. But then, you can manipulate energy, so maybe it is you. But I don't think it is."

"It isn't me," he muttered, an underlying tone of annoyance lacing his words. Great. I'd pissed him off.

"Well, Gran, said you were a powerful fae," I said defensively. "And you know, a powerful fae turned up at the same time as the orb."

"And you put two and two together and got five."

"Seems like," I admitted. Then he crossed the room so fast I could barely track his movements and touched his fingers to my cheek.

"You're too pale. Come downstairs and I'll make some tea. And then you're going to tell me everything."

And just like that, he was gone again. I frowned. He moved almost as fast as Monica, and she was a vampire. But he was right, I felt wobbly and a cup of tea sounded divine.

Downstairs, I sat at the kitchen table, with Archie on the chair next to me, and watched while Blake unpacked the box of kitchen supplies Gran had insisted I take. A starter pack, she'd called it. Bread, tea, coffee, sugar, milk, and various other essentials. *God love her.*

A headache was starting to niggle and I pinched the bridge of my nose, dropping my hand when a steaming mug of tea appeared in front of me.

"Don't know how you take it," Blake said, depositing a box of sugar cubes and a carton of milk in the middle of the table.

He sat opposite me and waited while I added sugar and milk to my tea and slowly stirred before taking a sip.

"Better?" he asked. I nodded. "Alrighty then. Spill."

I blew out a breath and considered my options. He was a lawyer, I could trust him, right? It had been Gran who had planted the seed in my head that he was behind the orb and that maybe he was involved. But today proved that to be false. So, I could trust him. I think. I squinted at him and he regarded me passively while I debated with myself.

"I think the best way is to show you. In my bookstore, I have this crime board..."

His eyebrows shot up. "You have a crime board?"

My eye twitched. "I do. It has all the information we've been able to gather so far and rather than rely on my memory—which, let's be honest, is a little swiss cheese right now, thanks to a certain number of shots last night—we should go to The Dusty Attic."

"And who is we?"

I frowned. "You and me." *Duh.* "You and me should go to the Dusty Attic to look at the crime board," I enunciated, slowly and clearly, figuring he hadn't understood me. Maybe I was slurring...I wouldn't be surprised.

He grinned. "No, I got that. Back up a bit. You said the crime board has all the information *we've* been able to gather."

"Oh! Right. So, that would be me, Jenna, Monica, and Gran."

He shook his head and I couldn't be sure if it was in wonder or resignation. "Seems you've got your own little murder club going."

"Don't call it that. Gran calls it that and it's not. You make it sound like we're ambulance chasers, and we're not."

He held up his hands. "Okay, okay. Not a murder club."

I finished my tea and glared at him. He smirked in return. Infuriating male. I carried my cup to the sink and rinsed it, leaving it to drain. It wasn't until I looked down at myself, thinking I needed a shower, that I realized something critical. I'd been flouncing around in my sweat pants, T-shirt, sans bra, all day. The critical words here were *sans bra*. The girls had been bouncing about, unimpeded, without me so much as noticing, not even once.

Heat scorched my cheeks, *again*, and I tried not to panic. I mean, he hadn't said anything, hadn't indicated at all that maybe I'd like to put a bra on. Oh god. Truly mortified, I tried to shuffle out of the kitchen, keeping my back to him.

"Harper? What's wrong?"

"Nothing. Um, I'm just going to quickly get changed, then we can go." I continued with the most awkward of exits from a room known to mankind.

"I didn't say I didn't like it."

Oh man. Just when I thought I was home free, he had to ruin it all. "What?" I squeaked in my chipmunk voice.

"The...view."

I shot up the stairs as if the hounds of hell were after me.

CHAPTER
ELEVEN

We gathered around the crime board in The Dusty Attic—Blake, Jenna, Monica, Gran, and I. Archie sat on my desk and watched the proceedings with a critical eye.

Seeing his name pinned to the board, Blake plucked it off and held it up. "Ladies, let me assure you I am not involved in this, other than as your lawyer, Alice."

Gran actually blushed. I blinked a couple of times, trying to clear my eyes. I'd never seen Gran look the slightest bit...abashed? Uncomfortable? Ashamed?

She cleared her throat. "Yes, well, I call 'em as I see 'em and you know, you turned up at the same time as the orb did."

"Let's find out, shall we? What's the timeline here? Harper?"

"Timelines are my job." Monica jumped up and, with vampiric speed, taped together pieces of paper and stuck them to the bottom of the crime board to begin the timeline.

"Kristen discovered Bonnie's body at around five," I said, to kick things off.

"I was arrested at seven or thereabouts. I remember because I was getting ready for my date. Such a shame I missed it because he was really dreamy too," Gran said.

"Yeah, we don't want to hear it, Gran." I stopped her before she could overshare. "I called Mom and Dad after Gran was arrested, but I'm not sure what the time was...I was a bit dazed for a bit and time got away from me. I think it was after eight? Maybe closer to nine? And then I went to Bonnie's house."

"How long were you there?" Blake asked.

I shrugged. "A couple of hours, maybe? Jackson arrived. We thought we could try and summon Bonnie, if her ghost was there, and that's when we saw the orb."

"And the orb was where in the house?"

"Upstairs in the attic. Next to Bonnie's altar."

"Not downstairs at all? At the crime scene?"

I shook my head. "Oh, and her grimoire is missing. I would have thought it would have been in the attic where Bonnie clearly practiced magic. But Jackson and I searched for it and couldn't find it."

"It's possible the police already have it in evidence," Blake said.

"But surely Jackson would have known that?" Jenna pointed out.

"I'll ask him." Before I could stop her, Gran had her phone out and was dialing. When he answered, she moved away so she wouldn't disturb us.

"What next?" Blake asked.

I stared at the timeline. Gran was in jail. Jackson and I searched Bonnie's house. Then...

"You arrived. I was back home, I'd just got in and you banged on the door." I said.

"I knocked," he corrected me. "That was around eleven," he said to Monica, who dutifully added it to the timeline.

I pointed at the timeline. "See? Gran was arrested at seven and you arrived at eleven, assuming my dad called you sometime between eight and nine, after I'd called him and Mom. How did you get here so fast?"

"Helicopter," he replied.

"Really?" Jenna said, voice full of awe. "That would be so cool."

I raised an eyebrow. "You hired a helicopter to fly down here to take on Gran's case? That makes no sense. This is small fry to you."

"The helicopter belongs to the law firm I work for. It's available for us to use. And since I'm friends with your dad, I said I'd do this for him. He was upset, stuck on the other side of the world, and he couldn't be here for you. So, I came instead."

Jenna coughed. "I'd hardly call being a partner in a law firm *working for them*."

"Let's not split hairs, hmm?" he replied. Damn it, he had a point. This wasn't a matter of if he was a partner in a law firm or an employee. This was to prove he wasn't involved in Bonnie's murder. But so far, all we had to go on was what he'd told us.

As if reading my mind, he held out his phone and we all squinted at the screen. "Flight manifest," he said. "The pilot logs all jobs in the case files."

Gran rejoined us. "Jackson's on his way," she said, clearly distracted with something on her phone.

"What are you doing?" I asked, watching as she held up her phone and took several selfies.

"Chap Snatch!" She beamed. "Isn't it wonderful?"

Monica slung an arm around her shoulders. "That would be Snap Chat, Gran." She looked at Gran's screen and grinned. "Oooh, he's hot. You guys should see this."

I rolled my eyes. Nope. Wasn't going to happen. Jenna took a peek and her eyebrows shot into her hairline. "Nice one." She high-fived Gran and I shook my head.

"Please don't encourage her!"

I took the sticky note with Blake's name on it from

him and tore it up, tossing it in the bin. He was no longer a suspect. Not in this case anyway. I still wanted to know more, like how he knew my dad. And was my dad the silent Jones in his law firm? So many questions. But they would have to wait—our number one priority was finding Bonnie's killer and clearing Gran's name.

While the others gathered around Gran's phone and sent Snap Chats to whatever hottie was on the other end, I pulled Blake to one side. "When Jackson gets here, something's going to happen."

"You're assuming he'll drop what he's doing and come running because Gran called?"

"Oh, he's on his way," I said, full of confidence. "Gran would have told him the murder club is in session."

"You said it wasn't a murder club," he pointed out.

"It isn't."

"But you just said—"

"It's what Gran calls it, okay? And that's not the point. The point is, whenever Jackson and I are together, in my bookstore, a ghost appears. I just want you to be prepared."

"I'm not scared of ghosts."

"Well. Good." I wish I could say the same because despite having the ability to summon Whitney without even trying, just the thought of a ghost sent shivers down my spine. You'd think by now I'd be used to it, but I doubted I ever would be. "Anyway, her name is Whitney."

"The Whitney Sims case?" he asked, and I looked at him in surprise.

"You've heard about it?"

"Came up in your Gran's research. So, she's haunting you?"

"Not exactly. She just likes to hang out. She's not malevolent."

I heard a car pull up outside followed by a knock on the door. "Here we go," I whispered under my breath, flicking the lock and opening the door to let Jackson in. *Five, four, three, two...*

"What did I miss?" Whitney floated down from the ceiling, heading straight to the crime board where she hovered, reading what was pinned there.

"Bonnie Emerson died?" she asked, shocked.

"Yeah," I replied, locking the front door again.

"I wonder who's managing her estate?" Whitney tapped a fingernail against her lip. "Her house is prime location."

Whitney had been the realtor for Whitefall Cove before her untimely demise. Now we had a realtor from a neighboring town visit once or twice a week to take care of any real estate needs.

"Can you talk to other ghosts?" Jenna asked Whitney. "Because those two"—she pointed to

Jackson and me—"haven't been able to make contact with her. Can you?"

"Oh! Well…I've never tried. I guess I could give it a go?" Screwing up her eyes and holding her hands out, palm up, then pressing her middle finger to her thumb like she was meditating, Whitney boomed out, "Bonnie Emerson! I'm calling Bonnie Emerson. Come in, Bonnie!"

I pressed my lips together to keep from laughing. Seconds ticked by. Whitney opened her eyes and glanced around. "Nothing?" she asked.

I shook my head. "Nothing. We think she may have already crossed over," I said by way of explanation.

"Okay then." She didn't appear phased. "Hey! Did you have the book club without me?"

"Book club got cancelled this week," Jackson told her, "due to Bonnie dying. Don't worry, you didn't miss anything."

"Oh good! I'd hate to miss book club. You said you'd hold it here so I could come." She pouted, then, losing all interest in us, she drifted up the mezzanine level and disappeared through a bookcase.

"Has she gone?" Gran whispered.

I shook my head. "Nah. She's reading." I'd discovered Whitney liked to snuggle in amongst the books, that it was her version of reading, and it suited me just fine.

"So, what's this all about?" Jackson stood with feet planted and arms crossed over his chest.

"We were putting together a timeline and it came up that maybe the police had Bonnie's grimoire in evidence," I said.

He looked at me, annoyed. "If we had it in evidence, I wouldn't have been looking for it."

"Whoa, dude," Monica drawled. "What's with the attitude?"

"What attitude?" he snapped. "You called me down here to ask stupid questions about a case that is, quite frankly, none of your business."

"Now listen here, sunshine." Gran stepped right up to him, tilted her head back to eyeball him, and wagged a finger in his face. "You weren't invited. You chose to come. And that's fine, you are always welcome, but don't you be telling me this isn't any of my business. "You"—she punched him in the chest with her finger—"arrested me. For. Bonnie's. *Murder.*" She emphasized every word with another jab to Jackson's chest.

Jackson wrapped his hand over Gran's and looked down at her, his face softening. I don't know what had gotten into him lately but he sure wasn't acting his usual self.

"You're right. I apologize."

"Accepted." Gran smiled and held up her phone for

him to see. "Have you ever talked to the lady in here? She knows everything! I think her name is Susi or something."

"Siri. Her name is Siri." Jackson chuckled, his eyes landing on me. We shared a smile before he looked away, his attention drawn to the clue board.

"Vernon Garza and Bernice Kemp were at the movies at the time of the murder. A double feature. Witnesses put them at the theatre," he said to the group in general, telling them what he'd told me the night before, at the ball. Monica put a line through both their names.

"That leaves Gladys Marquez and Kristen Lane," Jenna said.

"Gladys was home at the time. She lives alone, so no alibi. She had been over to Bonnie's house earlier in the day to deliver some eggs. She didn't hear or see anything at the time of death," Jackson supplied.

"What about Kristen's boyfriend, Cody? He seemed pretty angry when I ran into him and Kristen last night."

"Is he a witch?" Blake asked, and we looked at him. "Think about the orb," he said. "It's reasonable to suggest that whoever is using the orb is behind the murder. But keep in mind that it's an assumption. It could be a misdirect. Therefore, if this Cody person is a witch, does he have the power and skill to use an orb?"

"Gran, didn't you say that calling an orb takes a fair amount of power? Skill?"

"Sure does," she replied, distracted with her phone again. My god, she was worse than a teenager with that thing.

"So maybe your culprit isn't even on the suspect board?" Blake suggested. "I'd start with making a list of the witches who have the talent and knowledge for orb spinning, and start investigating from there."

"I hate to admit it," Jackson grumbled, "but that's a good point. This has to be magic-related. The grimoire has been stolen. Only a witch would benefit from that."

"What if..." I was thinking out loud. "What if whoever is using the orb is looking for the grimoire?"

Jenna almost jumped up and down with excitement. "Yes! That makes sense. The murderer kills Bonnie and takes her grimoire. And now...who? Who is using the orb to find it? Her coven?"

"That's where I'd start." Blake nodded.

"I'd start with the senior members," I said. "Gran said it's old magic. The younger witches possibly don't know about it."

"It could be a group thing, though," Monica pointed out. "You said the orb was brighter at your house, Harper, that it was dim at Bonnie's. So maybe the coven is getting together and putting in a group effort."

"Wait. The orb was at your house?" Jackson was appalled.

"Yes. And it moved like it did at Bonnie's." I mimed—as best I could—the orb, round and bobbing as it moved across the floor.

"And you're okay?" His concern was touching.

Until I said, "Blake helped me get rid of it."

"Of course he did," Jackson muttered under his breath and I narrowed my eyes. There was that jealous tone again.

"We need to ward your house." I'd finally gotten Gran's attention away from her phone. "Are we done here? Good. Let's go, Harper, we've got witch business to attend to."

I hid the clue board behind the bookcase, ushered everyone out, and locked up. Archie sat by my feet as I stood on the footpath outside.

"You go on home and I'll meet you there," Gran instructed, and despite her ridiculous outfit of a canary yellow tutu, fishnet stockings, black wellies, and an orange halter top beneath an oversized raincoat, she'd never looked more serious.

"Am I in danger?" I asked, and she paused from digging in her purse to look at me, her face softening.

"You're a little vulnerable, that's all, dear. Silly me, I should have thought that your new place would need a good cleansing and warding."

"Oh, it doesn't need cleaning. The realtor made sure it was cleaned before I moved in."

"Not that type of clean, love. We need to clear out all of the old energy. Even more so since an orb has been inside."

"Oh, you mean with sage and chanting...that type of clean." I nodded my head, finally understanding.

"Exactly. You go on home. I'll gather up the rest of the coven and meet you there in a little while."

I didn't argue. I was exhausted and a quick nap sounded wonderful right about now. "Come on, Archie."

Unlocking my car, I held the door open before sliding in behind the wheel. It felt odd not heading toward Gran's house but instead, in the opposite direction. The lighthouse stood on the bluff, the cove to the left and the township of Whitefall Cove tucked in behind the horseshoe-shaped bay. I had my own private road. No other buildings were out this way, and the public carpark stopped two hundred meters from my cottage, meaning any tourists had to walk past my house before they reached the lighthouse. Thankfully, the path wasn't directly outside my windows, so I still had privacy.

After parking my car in the garage at the back of the cottage, I opened the back door, turning to look at Archie who was now seated in the middle of the path, refusing to move.

"Okay, look," I told him. "I'll check, make sure no paranormal entity is inside first, okay?"

Meow.

Chuckling, I stepped inside, pausing to see if I could sense the orb in the house. Nothing. "All good," I called to Archie, who immediately trotted past me with his tail in the air.

After checking his food and water bowl, I stretched out on the sofa and was soon asleep, not waking until Gran was knocking on the door.

Struggling to sit up, I wiped the drool from my chin, checked to make sure I didn't have dribble on my shirt, then crossed to open the door. Lined up outside were Gran, Annie, Agnes, Jennifer, and Leah. The full contingent of the Sisters of the Sacred Flame Coven.

Annie carried a basket that was emitting tantalizing smells and she smiled as she hurried past me to the kitchen. "We figured you haven't had the chance to food shop yet, so we brought supper. By the time we've cleansed and warded, we'll all be hungry."

I glanced out the window, noticing the sun dipping behind the lighthouse. We had a couple of hours of daylight left—the day had gone by so fast, I'd lost track of time.

Agnes carried a sports bag that she heaved onto the table with a *clang*, before she unzipped it and started hauling out witchcraft supplies. Six bundles of sage. Six bowls. Pouches of herbs. Candles. Little plastic pouches of...stuff.

"Archie, go explore outside, but don't wander off, okay?" Gran addressed my cat. "I'm not sure this smoke is good for felines." Archie head bumped her shin before heading out the front door that stood open.

I rubbed my hands together. "So, what's first?"

"Cleansing! Getting rid of all the old energy," Annie said, handing us each a bundle of sage. "I want every corner of this house covered, from top to bottom. You know what to do, Harper?" she asked, as I took the sage from her.

"I think so," I replied. "Waft the smoke while chanting."

She nodded. "Close. First, light your sage bundle." With a snap of my fingers, a flame appeared, lighting the sage.

"Now, blow out the flame so all you have is smoke."

I did as instructed.

"First, we are going to cleanse ourselves. It's called smudging. Use your hand to waft the smoke over your body from your feet up to your head and then back down again. Repeat after me. *Air, fire, water, earth. Cleanse, dismiss, dispel.*"

We followed suit.

"Now I want you to spread out throughout the house, wave the smoke into all corners, across doorways, into the shadows, and keep repeating the incantation. Do not extinguish the sage. I want a bundle left smoking in each room once we're done. Take one of these bowls with you to put it in, so we don't burn Harper's new home down."

I headed upstairs. I was keen to smudge my bedroom, to make doubly sure any negative energy the orb had left behind was well and truly dispelled. Leah took the second bedroom and we both smudged the landing and bathroom. I left my sage burning in my bedroom while Leah left hers on the landing, with the bathroom and spare bedroom doors open for it to waft inside.

Back downstairs, the others were just finishing up. The windows and doors were open, and the smoke was drifting through the room. It reminded me of the dry ice at last night's ball.

Annie rubbed her hands together. "Right, now we need to ward the property. Harper, I'll need you inside. Sit over there." She pointed to the sofa and I dutifully crossed to it.

She handed Gran a feather. "Alice, you are air." Gran nodded and headed outside.

She poured sand into Agnes' outstretched hand. "Agnes, you are earth." Agnes joined Gran outside.

"Jennifer, you are fire." Annie handed Jennifer a

candle, who carried the lit candle outside and stood with Gran and Agnes.

She handed Leah a chunk of ice. "Leah, you are water."

I watched from the sofa as the four women began to walk the perimeter of the house, each of them chanting, depending on their element of air, fire, earth, water. "*By air, I ward thee. Guard this space from all ill will and all those who wish us harm.*"

Annie turned back to me. "Now, I want you to strengthen the ward. Close your eyes, palms up. Visualize pouring your energy into the wards."

I did as instructed, feeling it like a physical manifestation. Like a rainbow streaming through a window after a summer rainstorm, my magic whirled around the house, strengthening the ward forming, combining with my coven's and binding tight.

"Excellent." Annie beamed at me. "To maintain the ward, every time you come in or out of your house, I want you to lay your hand on the front door and pour a little energy into the ward."

"I can do that." I nodded, pleased with myself. This was the first time I'd used my magic in such a way. Lately, it had been spellcasting under supervision at Drixworths, and mundane stuff, like moving objects around. Nothing like this. This felt tangible, purposeful, and I liked it. I liked it a lot.

"This will keep the orb out?" I asked, stretching as the others made their way inside.

"Yes"—Annie nodded—"and anything else of a magical nature. It won't keep out a physical intruder."

"Hopefully it doesn't come to that," I muttered, before placing my hand on Annie's arm. "Thank you."

"You are welcome. We are family. Together, we are stronger." I liked the sentiment.

"Where's that food!" Gran demanded, stomping across the floor in her black wellington boots even though it wasn't raining—it wasn't even cold. With spring right around the corner, the weather was getting warmer and warmer every day. "I'm starving!"

I left the others in the kitchen, happily poking around in the cupboards and serving up the meal of roast chicken and salad, with freshly baked bread and a fruit platter for dessert. Stepping out on the front verandah for a quiet moment, I spotted Archie sniffing around the gate post, saw him sense my presence, and begin to trot toward me with his tail in the air. Pulling out my phone, I texted Blake.

"Have you heard from my dad?"

"No. Why?"

I gazed at the horizon, of the township of Whitefall Cove spread out before me—it looked like a postcard, a picture-perfect postcard. The sun was setting, and a riot of oranges, pinks, and purples streaked the sky, breathtaking in the display, bathing the town in an ethereal glow. From here, I could see the curve of the bay, could make out the dots of people strolling along the sand at sunset. And all I wanted to do was share it with my parents.

My phone ringing jarred me out of my musings.

"I said, why?" Blake didn't even give me the chance to say hello.

"Because I haven't heard from Mom or Dad since the night he called you. They were getting on a plane, heading home. That was two days ago."

"I'm sure it's fine. There are no direct flights from Australia, and if they're traveling at the last minute, I'd imagine there is a fair amount of plane hopping going on."

"Gran seems to think I'm worrying over nothing," I admitted.

"You should listen to your Gran."

"I guess." I lapsed into silence, my eyes still on the magnificent view before me.

Blake let the silence ride for a minute before asking. "How did it go? With the cleansing and warding?"

"Oh yeah, really good." I described the process and then felt myself blush. He was fae, I'm sure he was already very familiar with it all.

"What changed?" he asked, and I frowned. "You were all bright and happy telling me about the smudging, and then your voice changed. Why?"

He was far more astute than what I was comfortable with and I was scratching around for an answer when Agnes called out "Dinner's ready."

It was with a sense of relief that I blurted, "Gotta go, dinner's ready," and hung up. Hurrying inside, I closed the front door, rested my palm on it, and sent a little wave of energy into the wards before crossing to the table and taking a seat, smiling at the women who were indeed, my family.

"Great minds think alike."

"Jesus!" I almost jumped out of my skin at Blake's words in my ear as I stood in line to place my order at Bean Me Up the following morning.

With my hand pressed to my chest to still my thundering heart, I looked at him over my shoulder. Dressed in jeans with a dark sweater, he screamed bad boy. Maybe that's why I found him so irresistible?

"It's okay. I can wait until you're caffeinated and fully functioning as a human adult before we attempt anything resembling conversation," he teased, and I felt my face heat.

"Sorry. Good morning. How are you?" I said.

"I'm good. How are you? How was your first night in your new place?"

"Yeah, it was good," I lied. Truth be told, every little creak and groan the house made had jarred me from my sleep. I'd seen the dark shadows staring back at me from the mirror this morning, and despite trying to hide them beneath makeup, it seemed they were blatantly obvious because Blake whispered in my ear, "Liar," as his lips brushed my skin, making me shiver.

"Possibly." That's all I was prepared to concede on this topic.

"Positively," he shot back. Then it was my turn at the counter. I'd pre-ordered for Wendy, Gran, and myself, so our drinks were already in a cardboard tray. All I had to do was pay.

"Have a nice day," I said to Blake, leaving him at the counter while I headed toward the door. I didn't see Jacob Holt, but I felt him as we collided—he was coming in as I was attempting to leave.

"Oof!" I bounced off the door and felt it hit the side of my head as I staggered back, lost my balance, and toppled over. Oh great. This was going to hurt. Despite keeping a death grip on the cardboard tray, it nevertheless tilted and I sent up a prayer of thanks to plastic lids.

Trouble is, plastic lids tend not to stay on when the cups they are attached to drop from a great height. As I hit the ground, so did the tray. Three to-go cups bounced once, twice, and liquid went everywhere. It was at that point, as I lay there staring up at the ceiling and wishing I'd stayed in bed this morning, it dawned on me that my fall hadn't hurt. I'd been expecting a jarring impact. Then I noticed Blake, with his hand toward me.

"Protective energy?" I asked from my position on the floor.

"Indeed." He dropped his hand, releasing the force field he'd shielded me with. "You okay?"

"Totally fine, except for my dented pride," I said, sitting up and pulling my soaked sweater away from my chest. Thankfully, the drinks, although hot, had not scalded me.

"Shit!" Jacob exclaimed, looking at me in horror. "I'm so sorry! Are you okay? Oh my god, I didn't see you."

I laughed good-naturedly, my head only now starting to throb where it had connected with the door before I fell. "Not your fault, I didn't see you either." I let both of them help me to my feet when Jacob reached out a hand and touched my face. I automatically recoiled—what was he doing? Jacob was a witch, a member of The Crescent Coven.

"You're hurt..." He held out his hand, showing me the blood staining his fingers. I lifted my free hand to my temple and felt the damp stickiness of blood. Oh great.

"You're hurt?" Blake spun me around to examine my injury, pushing my hair back. "Napkin!" he barked at the barista, who dutifully handed over a bunch.

"It's okay, Blake, honestly," I protested, embarrassed at the attention. "Just a scratch."

"Yeah, and we know how head wounds bleed, don't we?" he teased, pressing a napkin to my temple. "Hurt?" he asked, not easing the pressure.

"No." Only a little lie. The throbbing had eased and it didn't hurt so much as sting. I brushed his hand away and replaced it with my own. "I've got this. Thank you, but I'm fine."

The door to Bean Me Up opened and Delores Lane, along with her granddaughter, Kristen, and fellow coven members, Bernice and Gladys, filed in.

"Watch for the mess!" I warned, worried someone could slip and hurt themselves.

"Oh goodness, Harper," Delores exclaimed. "Are you okay?"

"I'm fine." I waved away their concern. "Jacob and I ran into each other—literally."

"I'm so sorry." Jacob shoved his hands into the back pockets of his jeans and looked awkward. "I'll clean up."

"We all will," Delores announced and before my eyes, she cast a spell to clean up the mess on the floor. Only something must have gone wrong with her spellcasting because a mini cyclone developed, dragging the empty cups and cardboard tray from the floor and whipping them into the air.

"Oh no," Gladys whispered, "not again."

"What do you mean, not again?" Blake demanded, ducking to avoid being hit by a flying cup.

"Damn it," Delores muttered, trying in vain to control the cyclone that was picking up momentum. Napkins and salt and pepper shakers joined the fray as the cyclone traveled around the café.

"Everyone outside!" Blake commanded, ushering me out with a hand on my lower back. We all huddled on the footpath outside, watching through the window as the cyclone made an absolute mess of Bean Me Up.

Gran, hearing the commotion, came out of The Dusty Attic and crossed the street to where we stood.

"Delores tidying up again?" she asked, arms crossed as she surveyed the damage.

Gladys glanced at Gran, opened her mouth, but then snapped it shut and nodded instead.

"Here. Let me." Gran whipped out her wand, tapped the window three times, muttered a spell under her breath that I couldn't make out, and we watched as everything inside returned to its rightful place.

"That's how it's done, witches," Gran crowed,

tucking her wand into the waistband of her pants. "I guess you're wearing my latte?" she said to me.

I nodded. "And my coffee and Wendy's hot chocolate."

"I'm sorry," Jacob said for the third time, and I shot him an irritated look.

"It was an accident," I assured him. *Enough with the apologizing already.*

"Let me buy you replacements."

"Done!" Gran grinned and linked her arm with his. "I'll place the order, you can pay. Harper, I suggest you go get cleaned up."

Brilliant suggestion, Gran, thanks. But I kept the thought to myself, standing back to allow the members of the Crescent Coven to file back inside. Blake gave me a mock salute and returned to his spot by the counter and I headed across the street to The Dusty Attic, sans coffee, but now soaking wet with a bleeding head wound. What a Monday.

"Hey." Wendy glanced at the blood-stained napkin pressed to the side of my head. "Are you okay? What happened?"

"Bounced the door off my head," I joked. "I'm okay, it's just a scratch." I pulled the napkin away and tentatively touched the lump forming. It had stopped bleeding so I tossed the napkin in the trash. "Gran is getting replacement drinks. I'm wearing ours."

I headed into the bathroom that led off the

storeroom out back, dragging my soaked sweater over my head. The tank I wore beneath it was damp, but not sopping, so I pulled it over my head and held it under the hand dryer for a few minutes, getting the worst of the moisture out. Thankfully, it was black, hiding any stains. I really should go home and change but a book delivery was due in and I didn't want Gran or Wendy hefting heavy boxes around.

Peering in the mirror, I examined the cut to my head. There was a slight bump from the impact and a small scratch, which, of course, had bled like crazy, but it had stopped now. I dabbed at my blood-stained hair with a wet paper towel and was just finishing up when I heard Gran return with our order.

"Thanks, Gran, I've never needed this more," I said, pulling my coat over my tank and grabbing my coffee from the fresh cardboard tray that sat on the corner of Wendy's desk. Wendy picked up her hot chocolate and cupped it in her hands.

"Mmmmm, thank you." She smiled, taking a sip and rubbing her rounded belly. "This one is going to come out craving chocolate. I've been obsessed with it this entire pregnancy."

"There are worse things," I said, taking a sip of my coffee.

"Your mom liked pickles with strawberry ice cream when she was pregnant with you," Gran said.

I made a gagging noise. "Gross."

Gran drained her drink and slammed the empty cup on Wendy's desk. "Thanks for the latte, Harper, gotta run!"

Before I could reply, she was out the door. Judging by her Jane Fonda outfit, complete with leg warmers, I assumed she was going to some sort of exercise group. Or yoga. Or pole dancing. Honestly, with Gran, it could be anything really.

"Did you have fun Saturday night?" Wendy asked, leaning back in her chair and balancing her cup on her bump.

"Yeah." I nodded. "I didn't see you there?"

I cast my mind back, trying to remember if I'd seen Wendy or Bruce at the ball, but Wendy was already shaking her head.

"I wasn't feeling well so we decided to stay home."

"Oh no, is everything okay?" I was instantly on alert. Wendy laughed, waving me back.

"Relax, I'm fine. Pregnancy plays havoc with your body. My morning sickness comes and goes and lately, it's been mostly gone but it came back Saturday afternoon. In all honesty, I think it was a bit of anxiety about attending the ball."

"You and Bruce have been keeping a pretty low profile." I nodded in understanding.

"It's just so soon after Whitney died. People won't understand."

"Some won't. But others will. Don't let it get you down." I didn't really have any words of wisdom for her. After all, she'd been having an affair with Bruce before his wife died. It had been quite the scandal. With her death only happening two months ago, for Wendy to be pregnant on top of it all was even more scandalous.

"Anyway, I hear you had some excitement at the ball?"

Oh god, was she talking about the bachelor auction? I vaguely recalled bidding, but Jenna and Monica nipped that in the bud real quick. It wasn't as bad as it sounded. They weren't auctioned off for dates, not the raunchy kind anyway, they were auctioned off for chores.

"Your Gran stripped some guy naked?" Wendy prompted.

"Oh yeah. That." I shuddered, remembering the scene with Simon. Once again, when I'd expected to hear from him, I got nothing but radio silence. The whole situation was bizarre.

"So?" Wendy watched with anticipation written all over her face. "Do tell. What happened?"

I gave her the reader's digest condensed version and had just finished when the book delivery arrived. The rest of the morning was spent cataloging and tagging books and finding homes for them on the shelves. A perfect morning, in my book. If only I didn't reek of coffee and chocolate.

———

I fell into bed that night, blissfully exhausted, but even as slumber claimed me, my mind was on the Crescent Coven and the possibility that they were behind the orb. I mean, who else could it be? They were using the orb to try and find the grimoire—and they thought... what? That I had it? Did they think that I killed Bonnie because the murderer had to have the grimoire. The thought was sobering. Maybe they thought I was in on it with Gran—or that I'd possibly framed Gran. After our meeting with Delores, I'd thought we'd left on good terms, despite the practical jokes.

I tossed and turned, desperately tired yet unable to sleep. Probably because I was in a new bed, in a new house, with new sounds. Didn't seem to bother Archie much, he was curled in a ball at my feet making little snoring noises, while I lay staring at the full moon out the window.

Eventually exhaustion won out, and I fell asleep, but it was a disturbed one. Strange dreams, with magic pushing and pulling at me. The orb was here, bigger now, bigger than me, bigger than the house, and I was scared. I tossed and turned, mumbling in my sleep, then something changed, almost like an atmospheric change. What felt like pressure building now dissipated and, in my dreams, I saw a path of magic.

I followed it, flying along at dizzying speeds, like a rollercoaster, making my stomach churn. My fingers wrapped into the bed sheets, clinging on tight, but I didn't let go of the image. I followed it as we flew down the road into town, hurtled around a corner, down another street, zigging and zagging until I reached a house.

I didn't have time to check it out, to see if I recognized it, because I barreled through the front door, downstairs, and into a basement where a pentacle was painted on the floor, candles burning at each point. Sitting in the middle of the pentacle was a young man, and in his hand, a bloody napkin. His eyes snapped open as did mine. It was Jacob Holt.

I woke with a start, sitting up in bed with the covers clutched to my chest. Had that been real? It felt real. And if it was real, I was pretty sure Jacob Holt had seen me. He knew I knew that he was behind the orb.

Flicking on the bedside lamp, I grabbed my phone from the nightstand and called Gran, listening as it rang. After leaving her a voicemail, I tried Annie next. Hers didn't ring at all, it went straight to voicemail. Damn it, what was with these witches and their phones?

I had one more number to try.

"Y'llo?" Blake's voice was deep and sleepy. I'd woken him. But at least he'd answered his phone.

"Sorry if I woke you," I whispered. I heard rustling and did my best to block out the image that was currently playing in my head, of him sitting up in bed, sheets tangled around his waist, chest bare.

"You don't have to whisper, Harper." There was humor in his voice and I was relieved he hadn't bitten my head off for waking him in the middle of the night.

"Sorry." In the quiet of the night, my voice sounded super loud. Sitting in the middle of my bed, I kept my eyes glued to the door as if Jacob was going to burst through any second. Right at this moment, I missed the comfort of living with Gran, of knowing there was another body in the house. I was scaring the shit out of myself for no good reason. Well okay, a little bit of a reason.

"What's up, Harper?" Blake reminded me he was on the other end of the phone. "Something happen? Or is this a booty call? Because I'm totally okay with that." The drawl in his voice had my stomach flip-flopping in girly anticipation.

"Not a booty call," I said, and he chuckled.

"You sound disappointed."

"I know who's in control of the orb."

That got his attention. "Who?"

"Jacob Holt from the Crescent Coven. I had a dream. I saw him, in his basement, sitting in a pentacle painted on the floor, with candles burning, and a napkin with my blood on it."

Blake was silent for a moment. "You had a dream?"

"It felt real. Like a vision." I realized how insane I sounded, calling him in the middle of the night to tell him I had a dream that felt real. "Blake, I think he saw me," I whispered.

"This Jacob Holt...he's the guy from the café this morning, right? The one you collided with?"

"He is." I nodded, even though he couldn't see me.

"This could be your subconscious playing a trick on you, you realize that?"

I nodded again. "It felt really real."

"Okay, here's what we'll do. We will go and visit Jacob Holt tomorrow, see what he has to say." At least Blake hadn't written me off as a total nutjob.

"Thank you." My relief was evident. He'd believed me.

"You're welcome. Now, is there anything else I can do for you? Now that I'm up?" The insinuation was clear in his devilish drawl.

"Not right now," I squeaked, clearing my throat. "I'll see you at The Dusty Attic, if that's okay? Swing by when you're ready."

"It's a date."

"It's not a date. It's a..." I paused, fishing for the right word.

"I'll see you in the morning, Harper." Blake laughed. "Sleep tight."

Placing the phone back on the nightstand, I snuggled beneath the covers but didn't turn out the light. Sleep was a long time coming and when it did come, it was filled with dreams of being chased by Jacob Holt and rescued by Blake Tennant.

I wasn't sure which was worse.

THIRTEEN

Jacob Holt's house was just as I had seen it in my vision. Or dream. I'd given up trying to work out which category it fell into, I just knew I had to follow through on it, to know, one way or another.

"Ready?" Blake had picked me up from The Dusty Attic at ten and now we sat in his rental vehicle in front of Jacob's place. I'd grilled Gran about Jacob but she knew as little as me. Seemed a nice guy, he was the youngest member of The Crescent Coven, worked as a mechanic over at Exhausted, and rented a room in the big old Victorian house in front of us.

"You think he'll be here?" I asked, my gaze flicking from Blake to the house and back again.

"He called in sick to work. He'll be here," Blake assured me, opening the door and climbing out. I didn't ask how he knew he'd called in sick to work. There was a mysterious, almost menacing air about Blake today, which made me wonder if he'd always been a lawyer and what, exactly, had put him on that path. Was he a reformed bad boy? Had he once led a life of crime but was now on the straight and narrow?

With no time to ponder those particular mysteries, I climbed out of the car and followed. Last night, this had seemed like a brilliant idea. In the cold light of day, I wondered what on earth I'd been thinking.

"Come on, scaredy-cat," Blake teased, grabbing my hand and dragging me up the garden path. As soon as I set foot on the front stoop, I felt it. The energy.

"Can you feel that?" I whispered to Blake, squeezing his hand tightly.

"Yep," he confirmed, peering at the panel of doorbells. Six in total. He found the one marked Holt and pressed. I heard the buzzer echo inside, but no other movement.

"He's not home." I was half-disappointed, half-relieved, and turned to leave but Blake kept a hold of my hand.

"Wait," he commanded. He appeared to be listening, so I cocked my head and listened too. Faintly, in the distance, I thought I heard footsteps. Eventually, the door opened and a rumpled Jacob Holt looked at us through bloodshot eyes.

"I knew it would be you," he said. He looked awful, like he hadn't slept.

"And why's that?" Blake asked conversationally.

"Because I saw her last night. And she saw me." He pointed at me, his finger shaking.

Blake pushed his hand down. "It's rude to point."

"Sorry." Jacob was immediately contrite. Okay, so this wasn't as scary as I'd built up in my mind. In fact, it seemed that Jacob was just as wary of me as I was of him.

"Can we come in?" I asked. "Clearly, we have things to talk about."

All the color left his face and he swallowed audibly. "Are you going to kill me?" he croaked.

I looked at him in surprise, and opened my mouth to tell him that, in no uncertain terms, we had no intentions of harming him at all, when Blake muttered menacingly, "That's to be determined."

"What?" I whispered to Blake, who winked. Unsure what game he was playing, I decided I'd play along, for now.

"We just have a few questions for you. About the orb. That's you, right?"

"I didn't kill Bonnie," he cried, and my heart went out to him.

"Relax, kid." Seemed Blake took pity on him too. "We don't think you did. We want to know what you're doing with that orb and why you're spying on

Harper with it. For the record, she nor her grandmother killed Bonnie either."

Jacob visibly sagged, grabbing the doorframe to hold himself up.

"Oh, thank god for that." His relief was palpable and his demeanor totally changed. Holding the door wide, he ushered us inside.

"Let's go to the basement. I have it warded." Then he frowned at me. "Only you busted through."

"Err, sorry?" I offered, following him down a hallway, through a small mudroom at the back of the house that led to a narrow set of wooden stairs leading into the basement. It was pretty unremarkable, standard-issue type basement, if you didn't count the pentacle spray painted on the floor.

Jacob hurried to a pile of junk in the corner and tossed three milk crates into the center of the room. "Take a seat."

I flipped one of the crates over and gingerly sat down.

"When I heard that Bonnie's grimoire was missing, I got to thinking about ways we could look for it, track it. And I remembered my grandmother, God rest her soul, telling me about the orbs when I was a kid. I thought, if I could find that spell and make my own orb, I'd be able to freely search for her grimoire without anyone knowing," Jacob said, producing a dog-eared notebook from beneath a canvas duffle bag.

He flipped through the pages and briefly held the notebook out so we could see the page. On it, was a hand-drawn sketch of an orb. Ah, the tattered notebook was Jacob's grimoire.

"I take it you haven't found Bonnie's grimoire," Blake said, only sitting once Jacob had settled himself on the crate opposite me.

Jacob shook his head. "Sadly, no. I was hoping I could use the orb like a tracking device. Seems that wasn't the case," he admitted.

"Well, I can assure you, I don't have it," I grumbled.

"Sorry. But I saw you with Detective Ward in Bonnie's house. You were my only lead."

"I'm not even a suspect!"

"Well, your Gran is, and I couldn't get a connection with her. And then you turned the tables on me last night...what did you do?" His eyes were wide with curiosity. "I knew you'd warded your house to keep me out. That's why I took your blood, to try and break your wards, only I couldn't. And then you were here!"

Well, that explained what I'd seen, with him sitting with a bloodied napkin that he could only have gotten from Bean Me Up. I must have dropped one on my way out because I distinctly remember tossing one in the trash can in The Dusty Attic.

I glanced at Blake, who was looking at me with speculation in his eyes.

"I'm not sure. I wasn't entirely sure if it was a dream or real," I admitted.

"Oh, it was real. You were here, like, right there." He pointed to a spot on a floor. "Like an apparition. And then, *poof*"—He mimicked an exploding motion with his hand—"you disappeared. Scared the crap out of me."

"You and me both," I muttered under my breath.

"Well, Jacob, seems like you've learned a useful lesson, hmm?" Blake stood and we followed suit. "No more spying on people. You never know when it will backfire."

That was it? We were leaving? But then, I guess Jacob didn't have anything new to reveal to us. He was looking for the grimoire just like we were, and it seemed his only lead had been me and I certainly didn't take it.

"No sir," Jacob said solemnly, then turned to me. "But how did you do it? Was it astral projection? There have been whispers in the coven about you, about your power."

"I wish I knew. Sorry." I shrugged. All I knew was that I'd felt stronger, more powerful than ever last night. Maybe it was the cottage? Maybe it was the fresh wards and my magic was amped because of them? I had no real answers. But I knew where to get them.

After Blake had dropped me back at the bookstore, I called Izzy, the headmistress of Drixworths.

"Harper, how are you?" she answered on the third ring.

"Can I astral project?" I asked without preamble.

"Doubtful, but it's possible, I suppose. Why?"

I told her about what happened last night, how I'd traveled down the energy path of the orb to Jacob's basement.

"Ooooh, exciting!" I heard her clap her hands. "Come to Drixworths when you finish work. We'll explore this further."

I hesitated. "I don't want you to dampen my magic anymore. I want you to teach me to use it. To control it."

"Harper, I haven't been holding you back." She sounded puzzled. "Why would I even do that?"

"To stop me from going berserk? Like I did in East Dondure?"

"I think you learned your lesson from that little episode, don't you?" She was right. I had. Drixworths had stripped my magic and suspended my witch's license. That hadn't been a fun time at all.

"But you assigned Archie to me to help control my magic."

"That's what a familiar does, Harper. Helps control. But Archie can't stop your magic—he can help you funnel it, draw on it, but from what you're telling me, you don't need his help at all."

I frowned at that. "I'm not giving him up!"

She laughed. "Of course not. You're connected. He is yours and you are his."

"Right then." I huffed, calming down.

"Drop by after work, Harper, and we'll talk some more, I don't think you fully understand what is happening."

After work, I headed straight to Drixworths Academy of Witchcraft and Wizardry. The school was deserted at this time of day, with no elf to greet me at the door like there had been in the past. I pushed open the big wooden doors and bypassed the massive staircase in the foyer, heading down the hallway toward the back of the building where I knew the headmistress's office was.

Esmerelda Higginbottom—Izzy, for short—had taken me under her wing when my witch's license had been suspended and I'd been ordered to attend magic classes here at the Academy, and then re-sit my witch's exam. Thankfully, I'd passed the exam and had been meeting with Izzy every week since. I was technically on probation, but we'd also developed a friendship and I looked forward to catching up with her.

I knocked lightly on her door and pushed it open. Izzy was where she always was whenever I visited Drixworths, seated behind her desk.

"Come on in, Harper." She smiled as she finished typing something on her computer, hit the enter key with a flourish, and turned her full attention to me. "So, you're coming into your magic, eh?"

Her smile was warm and inviting. She was the type of person you instantly felt comfortable around. And slightly in awe of, not only because of her own personal power, but her goddess good looks.

"Is that what this is?" I asked, slumping in the chair in front of her desk. "It feels like I'm too big for my skin, like I'm going to bust out of myself."

"You've got this, Harper." She leaned over the desk, holding her hand out to me. Leaning forward, I placed mine it and she settled her other hand over the top, sandwiching my hand beneath both of hers. "I think you have denied your spiritual side for so long that you don't recognize it for what it is. A blessing. An extension of who you are."

I shrugged. Possibly. Although, I recognized a thread of truth in what she'd said. I'd been in denial with my magic for a long time, having stopped practicing witchcraft altogether when I moved to East Dondure five years ago.

"So, tell me what I'm capable of," I said now. "Everyone keeps telling me I'm powerful, and well, there has to be some truth to it since I'm one of the few who doesn't need a wand, but"—I paused, gazing out the window while I gathered my thoughts—"what does that really mean?"

"It means whatever you want it to mean," Izzy said softly, and I could have throttled her. She was an expert in saying plenty while saying nothing at all.

She laughed, reading my mind. "Okay, tell me what happened last night. You said astral projection?"

I explained what happened, the sensation between wakefulness and sleep, of zipping along the energy path the orb had left like I was an extra in *The Fast and The Furious*.

"Okay, take a breath. A deep one, in through your nose, out through your mouth...and...relax." She breathed with me. "It could be a form of astral projection, or energy manipulation. You don't have to put a label on it. What you did, you did instinctively. The orb invaded your space and you did what you had to do to protect yourself. That's not a bad thing, Harper. And you didn't use your magic in an aggressive or inappropriate way."

"I guess."

"Something else is bothering you. What is it?"

"It gets back to having all this power at my

disposal but not being able to use it the way I want," I said in a rush.

"How do you want to use it?"

"I want to find Bonnie's killer!"

"If only it were that easy." She steepled her fingers, resting her chin on top of them and studying me.

"How about finding Bonnie's grimoire then?" I was desperate. I was out of clues and out of suspects. I was confident that whoever had killed Bonnie had taken her grimoire. It was the key to all of this.

"Here's what you do." She leaned forward again, and I leaned in close. *Finally*!

"Meditate."

Say what? I sat back, looking at her like I didn't know her and she didn't know me. Meditate? My mind was like a squirrel on crack. There was no way I could sit and meditate! I opened my mouth to argue but she cut me off.

"Just try it before you dismiss it."

I crossed my arms and glowered. Of course, she took that as a challenge.

"Right. We'll do it together," she declared.

"What, now?"

"Yes. Now. Get comfortable. Both feet on the floor, hands in your lap."

With a put-out sigh, I did as instructed. "Now close your eyes. Take a deep breath in through your nose, out through your mouth, and as you exhale, all your worries and stress leave you, you are relaxed. And again, breathe in...breathe out." Her voice continued on, soft and melodic, issuing instruction, and I felt my body grow heavy in the chair.

We were around the point where I was consciously relaxing different body parts, I think we were up to my hips, when my mind wandered—as I knew it would. I started to think about our coven, of Gran, of Bonnie and what had happened to her. I pictured her that day, not knowing what was coming, happy in her kitchen doing what she loved. I imagined her delight at taking her angel food cake out of the oven, how pleased she was with it. I felt like I was there with her, could smell the cake, feel the warmth from the oven.

Then the image flickered, a quick snap of static, and I was back, standing now in the living room doorway, my back to the kitchen. Kristen rushed past me, anguish pouring off her in waves. I stiffened. This was it. Bonnie was dead. Had it been Kristen? I didn't see the act itself and didn't turn now to confirm that Bonnie was no longer alive, but I could feel it. Her spirit had gone. What caught my attention was Kristen running up the stairs. She said she'd gone out the front and called the police when I asked her about finding Bonnie.

I followed, making it as far as the landing, when Kristen rushed back down, shoving Bonnie's grimoire into her oversized purse as she hurried back down the stairs and out the front door. I stood, mouth open in surprise, then heard her on the phone to the police, her voice trembling with the shock and horror of what she'd discovered.

"Harper? Harper?!"

I blinked, dazed. Had I nodded off?

"What?" Rubbing my hands over my face, I shook off the dream.

"You did it, honey." Izzy was beaming at me.

"Did what?"

"You're not astral walking, you're having visions. Your spirit is moving through time and space. This is wonderful!" She clapped her hands in glee while I frowned at her.

"That was real?"

She was nodding madly. "Where did you go? What did you see?"

"I went to Bonnie's house," I said, voice flat. Her enthusiastic clapping and nodding stopped.

"Oh." *Yeah. Oh.* "And what did you see?"

"I need to go," I said, jumping up and scooping my bag from the floor. I was out and down the corridor, ignoring her calling my name. Outside of Drixworths, I sprinted for my car, fumbling for my phone as I ran.

"Hi, Harper." Jackson answered on the first ring. I liked a person who answered immediately.

"Jackson!" I exclaimed. "Kristen Lane has Bonnie's grimoire." I puffed, my feet sliding in the gravel as I skidded to a halt by my car, jamming the phone between my shoulder and ear as I dug around for my keys.

"She does? You found it?" he asked.

"No, I saw it. A vision. I'm on my way to her house now. Meet me there!"

"Do not approach her!" Jackson warned right before I cut him off, ending the call.

I couldn't say for sure that Kristen killed Bonnie, but she definitely took her grimoire and lied about it, and that made her look plenty guilty in my eyes.

CHAPTER
FOURTEEN

I'd had time to call one other person on the drive over to Kristen's house. Gran. She was the one they'd arrested, and the one out on bail. She had more skin in the game than me, so I figured it was only fair she knew. I hadn't counted on her getting to Kristen's house before me. Or having the rest of our coven with her. Seems the witch's version of the phone tree was working incredibly well.

Slamming my car door, I made my way to the group of witches who stood huddled around Kristen's front gate.

"What are you doing?" My irritation was evident in my voice. "Gran, you shouldn't have called them here."

"Nonsense, this is witch business." Annie sniffed,

her cheeks flushed. Oh, good grief, they were all primed for battle. I had to diffuse this right now.

"No, this is police business," I corrected her, "and Jackson will be here any second. I don't want you all here when he arrives."

I was promptly ignored. Gran unlatched the gate and began stomping down the path toward the front door, Annie, Agnes, Jennifer, and Leah following. I threw up my hands and hurried after them, pushing through to the front to stop them from mounting the steps.

"Wait here!" I hissed, holding my hands out, my back to the door. "I'll take care of this."

I glanced over their heads to the street beyond—where the hell was Jackson? He should have been here before any of us, but there was no sign of him.

I froze when I heard the door open behind me and glanced over my shoulder to see Kristen in the doorway, the Crescent Coven gathered behind her. *Fan-freaking-tastic.* This was going to get messy.

Swiveling on my heel, I opened my mouth to address Kristen when a swarm of bees descended. So, rather than demanding she hand over Bonnie's grimoire, I was instead flapping at my head, wincing as more bees than I would like managed to score a direct hit and deposit their stinger into my unprotected flesh. Our coven scattered and chaos ensued. The garden hose came to life, looping through the air, water chasing off the bees and dowsing the Crescent Coven mob who now stood side by side along the verandah, wands in hand. They were behind the bee attack!

Oh, it was on like Donkey Kong. Magic sparked through the air, as spells were cast and deflected by both sides. The shrub I was crouched behind went up in flames. I quickly extinguished it and frowned at Gladys who had her wand pointed my way. As I eyeballed her, Jacob shot his wand my way and a bucket of slime hit me in the chest. I glared at him and he grinned with an apologetic half-shrug.

"Eww!" I screeched. "So gross."

Gran saw the sliming I'd received and reciprocated tenfold. Only she didn't quite get it right and every witch on Kristen's property was now sporting a dose of green slime.

"Oops." Gran grinned.

The war of the witches was lighthearted, the spells harmless, if not messy, until the slats in Kristen's picket fence detached themselves from the railing, rose in the air, and came hurtling toward us. What the hell? My coven didn't see them coming but I did. Closing my eyes, I held my arms out wide and pushed a forcefield over us. The slats hit the barrier and fell to the ground.

Releasing the protective barrier, I squinted my eyes and tried to determine who had cast that particular spell. This was escalating and would get out of hand if it wasn't stopped now.

"What the ever-loving hell is going on here?" Jackson shouted over the din of a bunch of witches squabbling in the front garden. We all froze, and then all looked sheepish—myself included.

"Harper! Over here. Kristen? Over here. The rest of you? Clean this mess up," he growled, stomping to one side of the garden, clearly irritated. Jackson wasn't one to lose his cool often, so I quickly trotted after him. As I stood in front of him, he lowered his voice. "You told them? Why would you do that?" He ran his hand through his hair, messing the strands.

"I told Gran. That's all," I whispered, "I was not expecting the whole coven to be here. Mine *or* theirs."

Kristen made her way across the lawn to where we stood.

"I hope you're going to charge her for this," she snapped. "Coming to my home and attacking us."

"What?" I yelped. "You set bees on us. Look at the stings!" I held my arm out where three red welts dotted my skin. I knew I had more, I could feel them—they hurt.

Jackson grabbed my arm and looked closely at the welts.

"Definitely bee stings," he said, then looked to Kristen who shrugged.

"She could have got those anywhere. Must have disturbed a bee's nest in the garden or something."

"Show me this bee's nest," Jackson ordered, and Kristen's eyes darted around the garden, her face flushing with color. *Liar, liar, pants on fire.*

"Okay, fine. There is no bee's nest," she said sullenly.

"See?" I crowed. "She started it. I was coming here to talk to her! She attacked first!"

"You should all know better, grown-ass adults," Jackson muttered, running a hand around the back of his neck. "Let's get back to why we're here. Harper seems to think you have Bonnie Emerson's grimoire." He didn't take his eyes off Kristen's face. "Do you?"

"No," she shot back, and I looked from Jackson to Kristen and back again. Surely, he didn't believe her? I'd seen her take it!

"So, if I were to search your house, I wouldn't find it?" he pressed, his eyebrows raising in question. Her lips puckered together, and she shifted from one foot to another.

"You are so busted!" I couldn't help myself. Finally, a break in the case.

"Harper," Jackson warned.

"Sorry." I mimed zipping my lips closed.

"I don't give you permission to search my house." Kristen was grasping at straws, we all knew it.

"I don't need your permission. Just a warrant."

Jackson pulled out his phone and eyed her, his face cold. "You can make this easy on all of us, or I can make the call. What's it going to be?"

"Excuse me? Detective?" a voice called, and we all turned to see Jacob Holt hurrying toward us, a canvas satchel clutched to his chest.

"What have you done?" Kristen screeched, snatching for the satchel. Jackson grabbed her, hauling her back. I couldn't contain the grin splitting my face. Jacob had come through for us.

"I think this is what you're looking for," he said, not looking at Kristen who was twisting in Jackson's grip and issuing vile threats to him.

"Jacob has been looking for the grimoire too," I explained. "He's behind the orb we saw in Bonnie's attic."

"Is that right?" Jackson eyeballed him, then nodded at the satchel. "Open it."

Jacob did as instructed, flicking open the two buckles and pulling back the flap closing the satchel. Holding it open, he revealed a large leather-bound book.

"Take it out," Jackson ordered. "We have to make sure it's hers and not some decoy."

Kristen was squirming even harder now and Jackson snapped at her, threatening to put her in cuffs if she didn't behave. I thought she should be in cuffs regardless. He'd slapped them on Gran quickly enough.

Jacob pulled the book from the satchel and turned it over in his hands. There was nothing on the cover, no insignia or name to indicate it was Bonnie's, so he opened it, and there, on the first page...Bonnie's name.

"Let's go." Jackson took the grimoire from Jacob and began moving Kristen toward the gate and his waiting car. "We'll finish this down at the station."

"It's not what you think!" Kristen cried, tears streaming down her cheeks. "I didn't kill her. I just..." she choked, sniffing, then dragged in a sobbing breath before continuing. "It was a split-second impulse thing. I saw she was dead and...she's a head witch. Her grimoire would be priceless. So, I took it."

Nine witches stopped what they were doing and watched, open-mouthed, as Kristen was bundled into the back of Jackson's car and driven away. He hadn't spoken another word. Probably still pissed at the witchy war that had erupted before he'd arrived. I have to admit I was a little ashamed of it myself, and standing here with green ooze dripping off me, was a stark reminder that we were behaving like children instead of grown-ass adults.

I cleared my throat, getting everyone's attention. "Ladies. And Jacob," I added. "I'm sure you'll agree that this got out of hand. And we're all to blame. Let's get this mess cleaned up and behave like adults, shall we?"

"An apology would be nice," Delores snapped. I felt for her. It couldn't be easy watching your granddaughter be hauled away by the police. I knew exactly how she felt—I'd been through it when Jackson had arrested Gran. But Kristen hadn't been arrested. Yet.

"I agree," Annie replied, standing with hands on hips. "I'm waiting."

I rolled my eyes. Here we go, two stubborn witches about to go head-to-head—again.

"Let's just say all apologies are inferred and get on with cleaning up. Then we can all go home," I cut in before the spells started flying again. There was some grumbling, but it appeared they agreed with me because no more spells were cast. Now it was just cleanup.

Cleaning up wasn't nearly as fast—or fun—as the fight had been, but eventually, we were done. It was getting late, the sun dipping on the horizon, and I was starting to get chilled with the slime having penetrated my sweater, the tank beneath, and now my skin. I was dying for a nice hot shower and dinner.

"Have a good night, everyone." I was bustling Gran out the front gate when she stopped and poked her head around me to call out.

"I forgot something. Gladys, can I get some eggs?"

Gladys stared at us, hard. Then, without a word, she swiveled on her heel and disappeared into Kristen's house.

"Well that was rude," Gran said.

"You don't really need her eggs anymore anyway," I said, following Gran to her car and holding the door open for her while she slid behind the wheel. "The competition is over."

"Have you seen Gladys's eggs? The yolks are so deeply golden yellow and they are, by far, the most delicious eggs I've ever tasted. I don't want them for the competition, I want them for me."

"Ah, okay then." I smiled, kissing Gran's cheek. "We'll do a trip to the market. She sells them there, I believe." Gran nodded, then checked her watch. Seems she had someplace else to be.

"Bye, darl." She wriggled her fingers at me. "I've gotta get ready for my date."

I shook my head, watching as she drove off. Everyone else had left, and the Crescent Coven witches had retreated to Kristen's house. Most likely, to discuss what to do about their wayward witch who had stolen Bonnie's grimoire—and possibly killed her. All except for Jacob, who had followed us and now stood on the pavement while I unlocked my car.

"Thanks for what you did back there," I said, knowing it couldn't have been easy for him to betray a coven member. He shrugged, a sad smile tugging his lips.

"I wanted to get to the bottom of the missing grimoire, and I did. When word got out that you were headed here, I just knew that had to be why."

"I'm sorry." I shrugged, not really knowing why I was apologizing, other than that I could sympathize with his situation.

"Do you think Kristen killed her?" he whispered, his eyes sad.

"I really don't know. But taking the grimoire was a bad move. It makes her look guilty."

"You astral projected, didn't you? That's how you knew?"

"It wasn't really projection, more a vision. Like, I was there, but not. It was different than what I experienced with you—you saw me. When I had the vision of Kristen taking Bonnie's grimoire, she didn't know I was there."

"Couldn't you, you know…"

I knew what he was asking. Couldn't I go back to when Bonnie was killed and see who murdered her. A shiver ran over my skin.

"I don't think I can." It was my turn to whisper. "I think that would be too awful."

"It would, wouldn't it?" he agreed. "Plus, it wouldn't give Jackson the evidence he'd need. He couldn't arrest someone because you said you had a vision."

"Good point."

A gust of wind buffeted the car, making me shiver again. Night was falling and with it, the temperature.

"I've gotta go shower off this goo." I nodded at his equally filthy appearance. "You should too."

"Yeah. You're right. Thanks, Harper."

"Night, Jacob."

As I drove home, I called Blake through the car's Bluetooth. There was no answer, so I left him a voicemail asking him to call me. Then I wondered just what he did with himself while in Whitefall Cove. Technically, he didn't need to be here while Gran was on bail, he could leave and return when she went to trial. *If* it went to trial. Surely, we'd find the real killer before it got that far?

With those thoughts, my mind went down the rabbit hole of who killed Bonnie. Was Kristen the killer? It looked that way, but I knew better than anyone that appearances could be deceiving. I could not say with one hundred percent certainty that she had killed Bonnie. I saw her leaving the kitchen, yes. But it could have been as she'd said—that she had discovered her body and made that split-second decision to steal her grimoire. What wasn't clear to me was *why* she'd stolen it.

Archie greeted me at the door. He hadn't wanted to

come to work with me today, so he had spent the day at the cottage on his own. Judging by the rubbing, purring, and meowing, he'd missed me.

"Hey boy." I bent and scratched his ears. "I can't pick you up yet. I'm covered in slime and believe me, you don't want this in your fur. Let me take a quick shower, then I'll get us dinner."

Leaving my bag and keys on the hallway table, I hurried upstairs, stripping as I went. My bee stings still hurt and I knew I had to get the stingers out so, after rummaging in the bathroom vanity for my first aid kit, I found the tweezers and began the fun task of getting out each tiny stinger. Three from my arm, two from my face, one from my collarbone. Good thing I wasn't allergic or today could have ended a different way entirely.

After my shower, I dressed in my PJs, tossed a robe over top, and headed downstairs. The welts from the bee stings were still swollen and angry, but they didn't hurt quite so much. I was a little puffy in the face but I figured that would subside soon enough.

"Okay, Archie. What's for dinner, huh?" He'd followed me into the bathroom, had dozed on the bath mat while I showered, and was now hot on my heels as I made my way to the kitchen toward his favorite thing—food.

"How about chicken?" I asked, opening my fridge and remembering that I hadn't had a chance to grocery shop yet. "Or maybe not." I surveyed the contents of the fridge, grateful my coven had put the leftovers inside for me.

"We've got some eggs. And cheese. Sounds like an omelet to me." I glanced at Archie who sat at my feet, eyeing the contents of the fridge.

"You know you can have cat food, right?" I added when he didn't respond. He looked up at me with his big golden eyes and meowed.

"Omelets, it is." Taking the egg carton from the fridge and the remaining block of cheese, I quickly whipped up dinner, cutting a small portion off for Archie and putting it in his bowl. He purred as he ate.

"Mmmmm, this is delicious," I agreed, mouth full. "I wonder if these are Gladys's eggs? They really are flavorsome."

After dinner, I poured myself a glass of red wine and curled up on the sofa, remote in hand.

"What shall we watch?" I asked Archie when he jumped up onto my lap and began biscuiting my legs. I flicked through the channels, not really paying attention to the television, my mind on other things. Like, was it too early to call Jackson and ask him about the investigation? Would he even tell me what had happened with Kristen? Had she been arrested? But if that were the case, would that mean the charges against Gran were dropped? At which point, surely, he'd have told me.

I must have dozed off because the next thing I knew, I was jerking awake. Archie was gone and the TV was playing an infomercial. Picking up the remote, I switched it off and stretched, yawning.

"Archie?" I called.

His meow came from the back door and I got up to find him scratching at it. "What's up, boy?" I asked. "Something out there got your attention? I guess it can't hurt to take a look, but no running off, okay."

He meowed again and I liked to think it was in agreement. Of course, he could have been telling me he was making no promises.

I opened the back door and stepped outside, shivering a little. Archie darted past my legs and disappeared into the darkness. "Archie!" I called after him, so focused on my cat, I didn't see it coming. A whack to the back of my head had me seeing stars and sent me crumpling to the ground in an unconscious heap.

FIFTEEN

When I came to, I was tied to a kitchen chair and had the mother of all headaches. In the kitchen, Gladys was pacing back and forth, tapping a wooden rolling pin against her hand. I assumed that's what she used to crack me on the head with.

"Gladys?" I asked. "What are you doing?" I tested the ropes. She'd done a decent job—my wrists and hands were bound to the chair back and then the rope wound around and around my torso. I wondered if this is how she'd tied Bonnie up.

She swiveled to look at me, her eyes wild, her face pale.

"You shouldn't have done that to Kristen," she said, pulling out a chair and sitting at the table as if we were having tea. "Because now the police will look again. Look closer. And they'll see my mistake."

I had a sinking feeling I knew her mistake because watching the woman with the crazy eyes across from me, I was also picturing the crime scene. And she knew.

"It was the eggs, wasn't it?" She shook her head and ran her hand through her hair, making it stick up in odd angles that somehow matched the crazy in her eyes. "It was," I confirmed, certain now.

Gladys had left the eggs, complete with a note, after she'd killed Bonnie. Bonnie had finished baking, yet the egg bowl was full and the note was resting on top. The eggs were Gladys's alibi, and it had worked. None of us had noticed.

"Why did you kill her?" I asked, keeping my voice level, calm, when inside, I felt anything but. I flexed my hands, searching for give in the rope, finding none. I couldn't use my magic with my hands restrained and she knew it. Clever witch.

"I didn't mean to!" She shot to her feet, agitated. The chair tipped over and the crash made me wince. "Sorry." She righted it and pushed it in, resting her hands against the back. "She just wouldn't quit stealing the eggs," she told me, staring at the wall.

"Every day, she was over in my henhouse, helping herself. She didn't ask. She didn't pay. She just took what she wanted. She didn't care that I sold those eggs, that they were money to me, money I needed. I know it sounds silly, what's a few eggs? What difference would that make? To me, a lot. She was taking two dozen a week. That's a lot of eggs."

She stopped, swiveling her head to pin me with a look. Her gray eyes were as cold as steel, waiting for my response.

"That is a lot of eggs," I agreed, not knowing what else to say.

"So, that afternoon, when I discovered she'd taken even more, I went over to have it out with her. And she laughed at me. And *then*, she threw money at me. Said if I wanted it that badly, I could pick it up off the floor, as if I was trash. Then she stood there with her hands on her hips, waiting for me to grovel at her feet for the money."

Well, that wasn't very nice. Although, killing Bonnie was a bit of an overreaction.

"Of course, I didn't," Gladys went on to say. "Instead, I grabbed a saucepan from her sink and hit her over the head with it."

"What's your plan here, Gladys?" I asked. "There's no cake to shove down my throat. I haven't been stealing your eggs. Do I really deserve to die?"

I couldn't believe how calm I felt. It was kind of like waiting for the other shoe to fall—any minute now, it would drop and then I'd freak out. But in the meantime, I wriggled my hands again and tried to get my fingers free.

"If you'd kept your nose out of it, none of this would be happening. This is your fault!" she yelled, rushing around the table and slapping my face. My head snapped back, and my cheek was on fire where she'd hit me.

"Enough talking!" Her voice was laced with hysteria. "If you keep talking, I'll beat your head in with the rolling pin," she threatened, and I believed her. I didn't utter a sound, just watched her with wary eyes, my face stinging.

In the kitchen, she turned on all the burners and the smell of gas filled the air. She did the same with the oven, opening the door, so the fumes poured out. Oh good. I think I'd rather be gassed than have my head bashed in. Then I saw what she pulled out of her pocket. Matches. Oh no, not fire, please not fire. Not only me, but my beautiful cottage—it didn't deserve to burn.

Thank god Archie was outside. He'd be spared. My mind drifted to Gran, to Mom and Dad. I thought of Jenna and Monica, Jackson, and finally, Blake. It saddened me I wouldn't have another picnic with him, I'd never find out if his lips were as soft as they looked. I wouldn't relive the thrill of his hand in mine, or the heat of him as he stood next to me.

"What are you crying about?" Gladys snapped, and

that's when I realized tears were running down my face. I hadn't noticed. But one thing was for sure—I wasn't ready to die. I would not sit here and let her kill me, not without a fight.

"You're a coward," I taunted. "Killing someone over some lousy eggs? That's pathetic. And now you're killing me because I found you out? You're a chicken."

The mocking worked. She roared and lunged at me, her hands going for my throat, but I was ready for her. Using her momentum, I pushed down against the floor with my feet and we toppled over, crashing to the floor. Pain ricocheted through my spine and head, and my ears were ringing, but she let go of my neck to balance her hands on the floor and push herself up.

But I had what I wanted. One hand was free. The other was tangled in broken chair and rope, but one was free, and I used my magic to release myself from the rest of the rope. Her back was to me as she got to her feet. I saw her reaching for the rolling pin and knew what she intended to do next. As she turned and swung, I rolled, and she connected with the floor and not my head.

"Nooooooo!" she screamed, swinging again. I rolled back, avoiding the second blow. Bringing my feet up, I pushed her in the stomach, hard. She staggered back, not expecting the attack. I clambered to my feet, dizzy, my head throbbing. The air was thicker with gas now, making it difficult to breathe. I tried to think of a spell to contain it, but my mind was blank. I wasn't sure if it was due to a brain injury from two blows to my skull in a relatively short period of time, the gas, or something else, but my sense of self-preservation was high. I had to get out of here.

I made a run for the door, only I didn't get far as I felt myself being jerked backwards by my hair. Spinning around, I flailed with kicks, yells, and slaps, anything to keep her off but I'd misjudged. Gladys was strong for an old witch. She wrestled me to the floor, and I wondered if she'd been working out. I got a few more slaps in before her hands circled my throat and I began to see stars. And Gladys's eyes, crazed and intent on me.

My hand slapped around on the floor, trying to find something, anything, to use as a weapon. When my fingers touched something wooden and smooth, I reached my fingers out as far as they would stretch, wrapping my hand around the rolling pin. Channeling all my strength, I swung the rolling pin at Gladys's head.

I heard a scream. I think it might have been mine. As she fell off me, I sucked in welcome breaths of air and scrambled to my feet, staggering for the door and flinging it open to drag in sweet, sweet, fresh air.

Two police cars skidded to a halt, blue and red lights flashing, blinding me. I lifted my arm to shield my face against the unexpected glare.

"Take her!" Jackson shouted, pushing past me, but I stopped him, grabbing his arm.

"There's gas!" I gasped, coughing. "She has matches," I warned. Two uniformed officers were right behind him.

"I've got you." Strong arms swept me up and rushed me off the verandah. I clung to Blake, confused as to why he was here. With Jackson. Who had called them? He opened a car door and slid me onto the back seat. A furry head butted my arm, along with a familiar meow.

"Archie!" I pulled him into my arms, burying my face in his fur.

Blake squatted in the open door, his face full of concern. "He ran all the way into town. Pretty sure he was heading for the police station when I saw him."

"Oh, Archie, you good boy," I cooed, then I looked at Blake. "She's crazy. Please help Jackson. The place is full of gas and she has matches."

I blinked and he was gone. The adrenaline that had been keeping me going was fading fast and I rested my head against the back of the seat while Archie climbed on my lap and rested his head against my chest. I wrapped my arms around him and cuddled him to me, comforted by his purr.

Hearing a commotion, I turned my head and watched as Jackson and the two officers escorted Gladys out of the cottage, her hands restrained behind her back. She was ranting and raving—I couldn't make out what, it sounded like gibberish to me—and Jackson seated her in the back of the squad car before coming over to check on me.

"You okay?" he asked, leaning one arm on the roof of the car as he ducked down to look at me.

"Yeah, I'm fine. I've got a tough head," I joked.

"Tennant tell you that this cat of yours is the hero?"

"He did." I smiled.

"Glad you're okay," he said roughly, touching a hand to my cheek before straightening up. "See that she gets a checkup," he said to Blake before shaking the other man's hand and climbing into his car.

Blake leaned in and pulled the seatbelt across both Archie and myself, then gently closed the door. I looked through the window at my cottage, relieved beyond belief that it was still standing.

"What did you do?" I asked, once Blake had slid behind the wheel. "How did you stop her from sending it up in flames?"

Blake adjusted the rearview mirror and met my eyes. "I surrounded her with an energy field. If she lit a match, there may have been enough gas trapped in with her that she'd have gone up in a ball of flame. Although, I couldn't say for sure. Seemed she wasn't prepared to risk it. Once Jackson got the cuffs on her, I released the shield.

I've turned the gas off and opened all your windows."

It took too much effort to reply so I merely nodded and closed my eyes, the rocking of the car as we pulled away enough to send me into a light slumber.

"Harper?" Blake's voice blew hot breath into my ear, but I didn't have the energy to wake up. Not fully, and not just yet.

"Come on. We're at the hospital, time to get you checked out."

Right. Yes. I'll get right on that. In a minute. Just give me five more minutes and then I'll get up. Archie's warm body disappeared, and I grumbled in protest.

"Come on, up with you." Suddenly, I was lifted out of the car and cradled against a firm chest. It was almost enough to get me to crack open an eye. Almost. Blake's chest vibrated as he chuckled. Then the glorious dimness of outside was replaced by harsh hospital lights and I turned my face into his neck to protect my eyes from the glare.

The next few hours were a blur of being poked, prodded, stuck with needles, and generally not being left to sleep in peace like I so desperately wanted to do. Eventually, they decided to admit me and if it meant I could get some rest, I was all for it. After all, I couldn't go home, not tonight.

"Archie?" I croaked, forcing my eyes open. Blake sat by the side of my bed, watching the solution in my drip as it made its way down the tube and into my arm.

"He's fine. He's in my car. I'll take him home with me tonight."

"You can have cats in hotels?"

He shrugged. "I'm not really bothered with what I can and can't do right now."

"Are you okay?" I frowned. I was a bit spaced out—had he been hurt tonight?

He barked out a laugh, clasping my hand in his. "I'm fine. I'm worried about you, you nut. You scared me for a minute."

"Oh, sorry." I closed my eyes on a sigh. I was feeling better and not so fuzzy headed. My headache had gone, although my scalp was still tender, but I was still tired.

"What's the time?" I asked. He glanced at his watch. "Just after three."

"You should go. Get some sleep. Take care of my cat."

"I'd rather stay here," he grumbled.

"Please take care of Archie. He might poop in your car," I felt compelled to point out.

He laughed again. "A compelling argument. Okay. I shall see to your cat's needs if it will make you happy."

"It will. All I'm going to do is sleep. Come back in the morning and break me out of here."

"You can count on it." He stood, then leaned down and dropped a soft kiss on my lips. "Get some rest."

And then he was gone. With a sigh, I pulled the covers up to my chin and did as instructed.

Gran, Jenna, and Monica arrived the following morning.

"Ohmigod!" Gran sat on the edge of the bed and pulled me into her arms, her grip tight. God, had these witches been lifting weights or some sort of super workout? How did they get so damn strong? I winced a little and eased out of her grip.

"Easy there, Gran." I smiled, blinking a couple of times at today's outfit. Cut-off denim shorts with black leggings underneath, a floral slash Hawaiian blouse, with a striped, what looked to be home knitted vest over the top. Oh, and on her feet, blue bedazzled Uggs.

"You're all over the news. You're a hero," Jenna said with a little smile.

"I hope you got the scoop?"

She snorted. "But of course!"

"You could have been killed," Monica felt compelled to point out. "That witch was all sorts of crazy."

"Well, I didn't. I'm fine." I was dressed and sitting

on the side of my hospital bed, eager to go home. I kept glancing at the door, expecting Blake to walk through at any moment, growing more disappointed when the minutes ticked by and he didn't appear.

Gran clued in. "Blake called," she stated. "Said something had come up, asked if we'd give you a lift home."

Monica, dressed in her oversized summer hat, long sleeved coat, with scarf wrapped around her neck and face so that all that was visible was her eyes— behind sunglasses—and her nose, sat on the end of my bed. "He also said," she pointed out, "that he's totes sorry he can't be here himself and that he'll explain when he sees you."

"And Archie?" He'd taken my cat home last night and I missed sleeping with my feline companion. Never mind the crushing sense of disappointment that Blake wasn't here. Never mind that at all.

"He'll bring Archie up to your house as soon as he's finished with whatever it is that's keeping him away," Monica assured me.

"Don't forget he's a lawyer," Jenna pointed out. "I'm sure he has other clients aside from Gran. Maybe more complex cases too."

"Good point."

"Oh, good news on that point." Gran beamed. "Jackson called and said I'd been unarrested."

"What she means is the charges have been dropped," Jenna added.

"Oh, Gran, that's wonderful. About time!" I hopped off the side of the bed and hugged her, breaking apart when a nurse bustled in.

"Here are your discharge papers, Harper. Come back if you experience a return of any symptoms. Things like dizziness, nausea."

"I will," I promised, eager to get home.

"The bruising on your throat will settle, but if you have any trouble swallowing, or breathing, come back. It means there is swelling, and your breathing could be compromised."

I'd seen the angry purple bruises on my neck when I'd looked in the mirror this morning, but they looked worse than they felt.

We bundled into Monica's car, because hers had the darkest tint, and drove out to the lighthouse cottage. Having the windows open all night had done the trick, the gas had dissipated.

"We're going to have to smudge again," Gran grumbled. "The energy is all off in here."

Jenna put the kettle on and busied herself making us coffee while I perched on the edge of the sofa. "I can't believe it," I finally said, and three heads swung around to look at me.

"Believe what, love?" Gran asked.

"That it was Gladys. That she killed Bonnie. Then tried to kill me. It's so crazy and surreal."

Jenna handed me a coffee. "Did she tell you why she killed Bonnie?"

I nodded. "Oh yeah. Over the eggs. Bonnie kept sneaking into her chicken coop and stealing the eggs. And that day, it just tipped Gladys over the edge."

"Crazy chicken lady," Monica declared, accepting the coffee Jenna held out to her.

We all heard a car pull up outside and I jumped to my feet, hoping it was Blake with Archie. Opening the front door, I smiled when I recognized Blake's rental car. He opened the door and Archie leaped out, trotting toward me, meowing all the way. I bent and scooped him into my arms.

"I missed you too, boy." I kissed his nose and held him tight while watching Blake walk toward me.

His dark eyes swept me from head to toe.

"Hi," I said, trying for sexy but nailing chipmunk once again.

"Hi yourself," he said, his voice low and smooth. He tucked my hair behind one ear, his fingers brushing against my cheek. "We have to talk, but first..."

Then he kissed me. Boy, did he kiss me.

Archie sprang out of my arms, freeing me to pull Blake closer and run my fingers through his hair. The kiss went on forever but ended all too soon.

"What's wrong?" I whispered, his face giving him

away. Something was terribly, terribly wrong, and try as he might to hide it, I could see the truth.

Blake took hold of my hands and looked deep into my eyes.

"Harper...it's about your parents."

My heart stopped. I closed my eyes for a second as a million wild ideas ricocheted around in my bruised brain. When I opened them again, Blake was watching me intently.

"Tell me." I braced myself. One part of me hoped this was some elaborate joke, that he was about to yell "surprise," and they'd leap out from the back seat of the car. I even snuck a look over his shoulder, but I couldn't see through the tinted glass.

"Harper, your parents are missing. They missed their flight in Adelaide. No one knows where they are."

It was one of those moments where everything freezes and then comes at you at a million miles an hour. I kept my eyes locked on his, drawing on his strength, willing myself to remain calm.

"Right," I finally said. "Looks like we're going to Australia."

Ready to read Harper's next adventure in **Witch Way Down Under**? *Get your copy here:*
www.JaneHinchey.com/DownUnder

Thank you for reading! If you enjoyed this book, I'd greatly appreciate your review.

You can find a complete list of my books, including series and reading order on my website at:

www.JaneHinchey.com

Join my newsletter here:

www.JaneHinchey.com/subscribe

And finally, join my readers group on Facebook here:

www.JaneHinchey.com/LittleDevils

Thank you so much for taking a chance and reading my book . It's readers like you who make this journey worthwhile and fuel my passion for storytelling. Your support means the world to me, and I can't wait to share more exciting stories with you in the future.

xoxo

Jane

FREE BOOK OFFER

Want to get an email alert when a new book is released?

Sign up for my newsletter today,

https://janehinchey.com/subscribe

and as a bonus, receive a FREE e-book of

Cupcakes & Curses!

READ MORE BY JANE

Find them all at www.JaneHinchey.com/books

<u>The Ghost Detective Mysteries</u>

#1 Ghost Mortem

#2 Give up the Ghost

#3 The Ghost is Clear

#4 A Ghost of a Chance

#5 Here Ghost Nothing

#6 Who Ghost There?

#7 Wild Ghost Chase

#8 Easy Come, Easy Ghost

#9 Life Ghost On

<u>Witch Way Paranormal Cozy Mystery Series</u>

#1 Witch Way to Magic & Mayhem

#2 Witch Way to Romance & Ruin

#3 Witch Way Down Under

#4 Witch Way to Beauty & the Beach

#5 Witch Way to Death & Destruction

#6 Witch Way to Secrets & Sorcery

<u>**The Gravestone Mysteries**</u>

#1 Fur the Hex of it

#2 Battle of the Hexes

#3 What the Hex

<u>**The Midnight Chronicles**</u>

#1 One Minute to Midnight

#2 Two Minutes Past Midnight

#3 Third Strike of Midnight

<u>**Clean Scene Inc.**</u>

#1 All in Vein

PARANORMAL ROMANCE/URBAN FANTASY

The Awakening Trilogy

Hell's Angel Trilogy

The Enforcer Series (4 books)

Standalones

Returned

Secret Fates

Destiny's Touch

Blood Cursed

Heart of Darkness

About Jane

Hi there! I'm Jane, crafting tales of paranormal cozy mysteries sprinkled with urban fantasy romance. Between sips of coffee and dodging my mischievous cats, I immerse myself in stories where magic meets everyday life.

Once known as Zahra Stone in the world of steamy urban fantasy, I've now merged those fiery tales under the Jane Hinchey banner. Off the page you'll find me binging on true crime documentaries or sneaking in a Power Nap. Dive into my stories and join me on an enchanting journey!

Find me here: www.janehinchey.com

facebook.com/janehincheyauthor

instagram.com/janehincheyauthor

amazon.com/Jane-Hinchey/e/B0193449MI

bookbub.com/authors/jane-hinchey

goodreads.com/jane_hinchey

www.ingramcontent.com/pod-product-compliance
Lightning Source LLC
Chambersburg PA
CBHW030638110726
47901CB00002B/490